BY JAMIE EDMUNDSON

ME THREE
Og-Grim-Dog: The Three-Headed Ogre
Og-Grim-Dog and The Dark Lord
Og-Grim-Dog and The War of The Dead
Og-Grim-Dog: Ogre's End Game

THE WEAPON TAKERS SAGA
TORIC'S DAGGER
BOLIVAR'S SWORD
THE JALAKH BOW
THE GIANTS' SPEAR

Og-Grim-Dog: The Three-Headed Ogre

JAMIE EDMUNDSON

Og-Grim-Dog: The Three-Headed Ogre
Book I of Me Three
Copyright © 2020 by Jamie Edmundson.
All rights reserved.
First Edition: 2020

ISBN 978-1-912221-06-6

Author website jamieedmundson.com

Cover Artwork: Andrey Vasilchenko

No part of this book may be reproduced, scanned, or distributed in any printed or electronic form without permission. Please do not participate in or encourage piracy of copyrighted materials in violation of the author's rights. Thank you for respecting the hard work of this author.

This is a work of fiction. Names, characters, places, and incidents either are the product of the author's imagination or are used fictitiously, and any resemblance to locales, events, business establishments, or actual persons—living or dead—is entirely coincidental.

For Maria

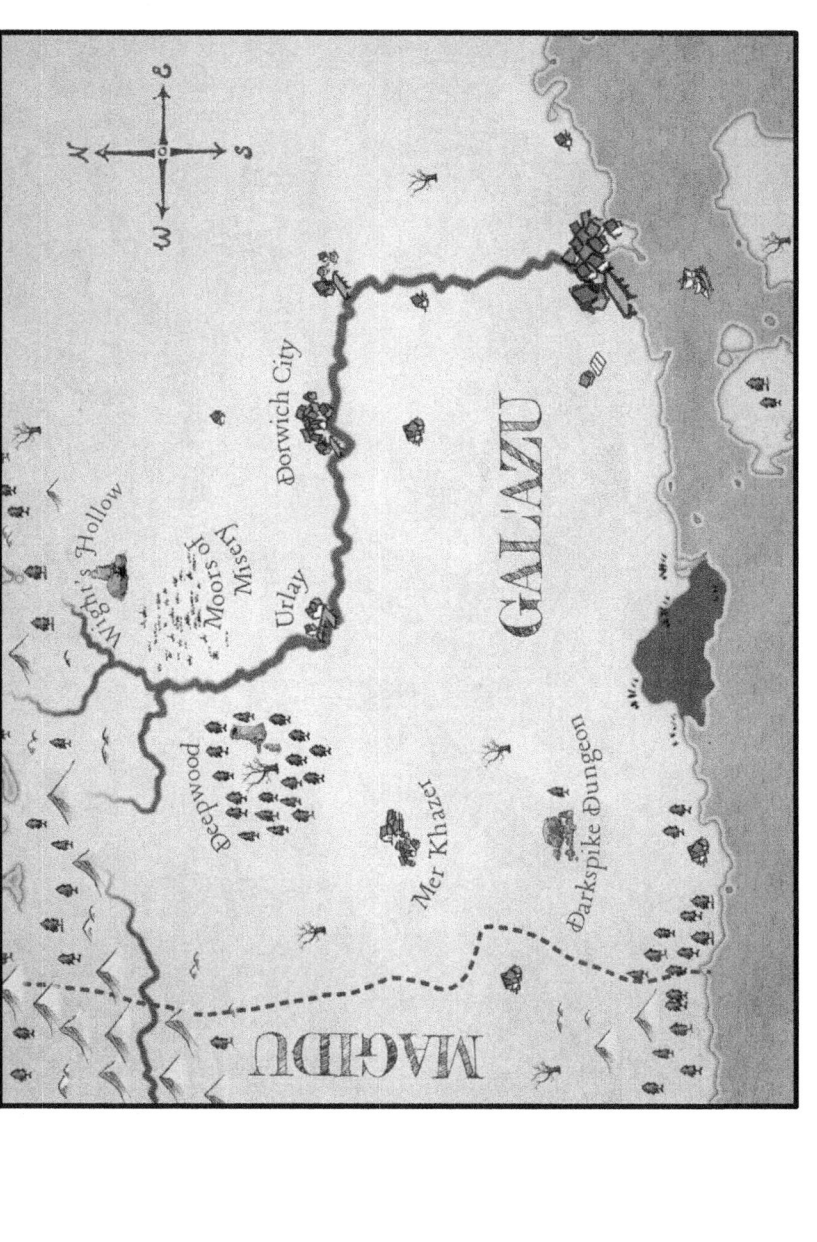

AN OGRE OF THREE HEADS

It was night-time at the Flayed Testicles. Drinking time.

Conversation swirled around the inn, laughter erupting from one corner, dark and secret mutterings in another. Men and women talking and drinking, with nowhere better to be and nothing better to do. You could say it was an inn like any other in the land of Magidu.

Except for the landlord.

Tea towel permanently draped over one shoulder, he was the oil that kept the wheels turning, serving food and drink with cheery amiability, a dirty joke for the women and a wink for the men. Respectful yet familiar; controlled yet approachable. And no-one ever tried to make trouble in his inn. For he was an ogre, and he was an ogre of three heads.

It could have been awkward addressing an ogre of three heads. Which pair of eyes to look at? Use one name or all three? But this ogre insisted on being called Landlord, and Landlord only. And if you called out this name, then invariably you found three pairs of eyes all looking your way, each head giving you their undivided attention.

And so it was that this night, the regulars called out this name, a name that was not really a name at all. No longer demanding to be served his ale, though that would continue to flow all night, never fear. They demanded something they had found to be even more valuable, and something never watered down, either. They called out for a story. For, in the quiet and peaceable backwater that was Magidu, they loved a bloodcurdling story, and no-one told a story quite as peculiar, or marvellous, or chilling, as the Landlord. The Landlord's stories were outlandish, outrageous, preposterous, completely unbelievable. Yet, when he told them, the Landlord's customers all agreed it sounded like he had been there himself. This, they would tell each other, is the mark of a truly great storyteller. Not to mention, with three heads, he was very good at doing all the voices.

The conversations died down, the anticipation heightened. The Landlord took his time wiping down the bar, letting the tension build as all great performers know to do.

But this night would be different from all the other nights.

It wasn't because of the Landlord or his regulars. It was because of a newcomer.

Sitting at the table at the front of the inn was a small, bespectacled man. His clothing was old-fashioned and worn-looking. It had the effect of making him look older than he really was.

As the Landlord wiped at his bar, getting ready to begin, he couldn't help but notice that large segments of his audience were distracted. People were gesturing at the man on the front table, a quill in one hand hovering over a piece of parchment, apparently ready to record whatever words might be emitted from the Landlord's mouths.

The genial mask slipped somewhat.

'What are you doing?' asked one of the heads.

'I intend to record what you say,' answered the man matter-of-factly.

'Why would you do that?' asked a second head.

'Because I know who you are. You are Og-Grim-Dog.'

Gasps erupted around the inn. A name—they had a name. No longer the Landlord, this ogre was Og-Grim-Dog, one name for each head, together forming a whole.

'You must have me mistaken,' said the second head.

'Mistaken?' asked the man, the pitch of his voice rising at the end of the word. 'How many three-headed ogres are there?' he said, a little smugly.

'You'd be surprised,' suggested the third head.

'Come on,' said the man in a chiding voice, wafting his quill at the ogre. 'You are Og-Grim-Dog, infamous across Gal'azu.'

The regulars at the Testicles muttered at this. Had their Landlord really come here from Gal'azu—the dangerous, edgier province to the east? Could it be? Could it be that his stories, so fanciful and fantastical, were episodes from his previous life?

'Everyone in my homeland knows at least one story about your exploits,' continued the newcomer. 'But I have travelled here to find out the truth. To sift the facts from the fabrications, to peel back the layers of myth-making, the exaggeration and the misrepresentation; to record for posterity, what really happened. Once I have done my work, broken in and bridled the fable with my tools—this quill, this ink, and this parchment—I will have copies made and distributed, so that all may know the truth of it.'

'You dare to make such a claim?' demanded the Landlord's first head, in a deep growl of a voice that none here had ever heard before. The ogre before them seemed to grow, and the Testicles shrank. As if awakening from a stupor, or a spell, they could see the hard, grey skin; the giant teeth; the thick black hairs sprouting from knobbly warts. And it was only then that the regulars of the Flayed Testicles recognised their terrible folly, of frequenting an inn owned by a three-headed ogre.

'You, with your puny tools, a feather and a small bottle of ink, will break and shackle our legend? We are Og-Grim-Dog! We have been loved and reviled! We have been the Hero of the Hour, the Darkest Villain, and everything in between! We have saved this world and travelled to worlds beyond it! We have deployed weapons of death beyond your imagination! They have called us The Destroyer! The Unclassifiable! We graduated top of our class in Rhetoric! We once shagged a—'

The second head coughed. 'Remember, we agreed not to mention that,' it said under its breath.

'Oh yes, sorry,' replied head one. It turned back to the man, a mean and fiery look in its eyes. It opened its mouth, revealing its teeth, each the size of a human's hand. It made its hand into a fist, the size of a human's head. The newcomer crumpled under the glare and the hostility and the threat of imminent, bloody violence. 'You think you can distil the life of Og-Grim-Dog into some words on a page?'

The inn became silent. It was the silence of a question left hanging in the air.

'Maybe,' squeaked the man.

The silence transmuted, to the sound of the Flayed Testicles holding its collective breath. They hadn't come out tonight to watch a man be torn apart and eaten in three separate, ogre-sized mouths. Having said that, it would be something to tell the grandchildren…

'Very well,' said the ogre, in a surprisingly calm voice. 'You accept the challenge. But know this. Failure on your part will result in not only your death, but the death of every man, woman and under-age drinker in this inn.'

A third silence. The silence when everyone thinks to themselves, *I could have stayed at home tonight.*

'Agreed,' said the stranger, apparently entirely comfortable about risking the lives of all present.

The regulars of the Testicles stared at the man with antipathy, but he seemed oblivious. He dipped his quill into his ink pot and held it at the ready. 'Where shall we start?' he asked.

'Let's start in the middle,' suggested the ogre's third head.

'Why the hell would we start there?' demanded the first head angrily.

'A non-linear narrative is more flamboyant,' explained the third head.

'More pretentious,' countered the first.

'It's also a better stylistic choice for this project,' continued the third head, warming to the subject, 'which is based on our recall of our collective memories.'

The newcomer scrunched his face up at this and shook his head. 'I don't know. That approach is going to make it a lot harder for me.'

The Flayed Testicles looked anxiously from the man's troubled expression to the ogre's first head. Anything that made the task harder for the Recorder made their deaths more likely.

The ogre smiled—a sly, self-satisfied kind of smile.

'Then the middle it is.'

DARKSPIKE DUNGEON

'Are you Og-Grim-Dog, the three-headed ogre?' asked the goblin.

'D'ya see any other three-headed ogres round here?' asked Dog, rather impolitely.

Grim sighed. There was no need to be rude, and sarcasm was wasted on goblins. It was now looking around the cavern for other three-headed ogres. Dog barked with laughter at the creature's confusion.

But there was no-one else in the cavern, and barely any furniture. A wooden chest stood against one wall, a weapons rack on another. In one corner was the ogre's pile of bones.

'Yes, that's us,' said Grim. 'Gary, isn't it?'

The goblin grinned, pleased that Grim knew his name.

'I bring a message from—'

'Wait. Wait a moment,' interrupted Dog. 'Your name is Gary? Why, by the twenty-three circles of fiery Gehenna, is your name Gary?'

Grim felt Og wake from his snooze next to him.

'Stop persecuting Gary!' Og demanded drowsily.

'Persecuting him? I'm not persecuting him, I'm just asking why he has changed his name. He had a perfectly good name. What was your name, son?' he asked the goblin.

'Grarviaksrurm,' the goblin answered promptly.

'Exactly! Perfectly good name,' said Dog, though Grim detected a hint of doubt in his voice now. 'A perfectly good goblin name. Gary just sounds ridiculous.'

'He's changed his name,' said Og, now fully awake and getting louder, 'because goblins are discriminated against! The system has forced him to take a human name. Don't blame the victim!'

'System? Victim? What the—'

'Yes, victim! You're just perpetuating—'

'SILENCE!' shouted Grim.

This always happened when Og and Dog had an argument. They shouted at each other, but since Grim was the middle head, they actually both shouted at him. He was sure he was going deaf as a result.

'Gary says he has a message for us, so I think we should find out what it is.'

'The orcs want to see you. Immediately.'

'The orcs?' Dog asked, making a face. 'If the orcs want to see us, why don't they come ask us themselves?'

'Exactly!' said Og, as if he had just won their argument.

'Please,' said Grim, trying to forestall further shouting. 'Why don't we just go and see what's up?'

Og-Grim-Dog followed Gary out of their cavern and up the gently rising stone path that linked their home to the rest of Darkspike Dungeon.

Most of this part of the dungeon had been formed naturally: the stone walls were rough and untreated, the ceilings damp with water, so that there was a constant dripping noise, whether day or night. It was a lovely part of the world, and Og-Grim-Dog had made sure that no-one else was tempted to share it with them. Indeed, if you ignored the noise from the kobolds upstairs, it was a very peaceful place to live.

Up they went, to the next level of the dungeon. Here, things were more hectic. It was a densely populated area, full of orcs, goblins and trolls, or 'green-skins' as Dog called them. Grim didn't use the term, since Og insisted it was racist. They did all have green skin, though.

Gary led them through the dimly lit corridors, past rooms full of goblin warriors, who peered out at them suspiciously. They negotiated the dungeon traps that had been set here and there to catch out unwary trespassers. The smell of blood came on the air: freshly slaughtered meat. Grim's mouth watered and the ogre's stomachs rumbled.

They came upon a scene of violence and destruction. Doors had been smashed off hinges, splinters of wood everywhere. The clean-up operation had begun, but many orc bodies still lay sprawled where they had fallen. Elsewhere, ribbons of blood and guts, in shades of red and brown, glistened on the ground where bodies had been dragged away.

Amidst the carnage, hands on hips, stood Krim, the Orc Queen. Seeing Og-Grim-Dog, she waved them over.

'Thanks, goblin,' she said to Gary, giving him a little trinket before waving him away.

She cleared her throat noisily, and for some time, until an orc standard-bearer, flustered looking, rushed over to her side.

'Way to make me look stupid,' she said sourly. 'Get on with it, then.'

'Her Exalted Royal Majesty, Sovereign and Despot of the Black Orcs of Darkspike Dungeon, Overlord of the Orc Nation!' he declared in a powerful voice.

'Really, Krim?' asked Dog. 'What's with all this pompous flimflam?'

'It may be flimflam,' she conceded. 'But it is high time we learned a thing or two from the humans. They've been giving themselves ludicrous titles for centuries. And now their people just believe it all. And obey. Why shouldn't I do the same?'

'Why does everyone want to behave like the humans?' Dog demanded.

'Because they're winning,' said Krim. 'Look around you. Another attack—my soldiers slain, any treasures we had left taken. We orcs are done. There's not enough of us left to even give them a fight next time it happens. And that means they'll come after the rest of you. It's orcs who are dying right now, but don't think you'll be spared.'

'Well, leaving your treasure lying around doesn't help for starters,' said Dog. 'You're inviting trespassers down here.'

'You've done it again!' Og shouted, into Grim's ear. 'Blaming the victims. That's twice in a matter of minutes!'

'But that's just it,' said Krim, mercifully cutting off another argument. 'There was nothing left to take. I haven't had enough fit and healthy warriors to go out raiding for months. The humans must have known that. They took all we had left the last time they attacked. They didn't come down here to win treasure. They came to kill us.'

'Hmm,' said Grim. 'Trespassing down here to find treasure we stole from them is one thing. But coming with the sole purpose of murder is quite another. But what should we do about it? More traps and stronger defences aren't doing the trick.'

'Someone needs to go up there,' said Krim. 'Find out what is going on, who's behind it, and why. I'd try myself, but I'm up to my neck in it here. Besides, the humans kill orcs on sight now.

Quite frankly, it needs to be you. You're the only other person in this dungeon with the brains to do it.'

Ogres are stubborn, bull-headed creatures. Abduct their mother, threaten her with all kinds of torture and they'll offer to do it themselves, just so no-one thinks they're a pushover.

But flattery. That works every time.

A DRINK AT THE BRUISED BOLLOCKS

Og-Grim-Dog left Darkspike Dungeon and went travelling in the Great Outside. There were no comforting grey stone walls and ceilings here, closing in on them, keeping the air just the right side of stale. Instead there was the wide, blue sky that stretched out in every direction. It stretched upward, as far as the eye can see, and then farther still. Grim tried not to think about it.

There was a certain system Og-Grim-Dog had developed when it came to travelling in the Great Outside. To understand it, we must briefly mention limbs. Og-Grim-Dog had two arms and two legs. The left and right heads, Og and Dog, had use of one arm each. Grim had use of the legs. It was a roughly fair division, even though it had its problems from time to time.

At Og-Grim-Dog's belt, wrapped around a huge waist, hung two weapons. Close to Og's arm was a pike. It was actually a human pike that Og had come by and rather liked. But whereas humans were required to hold the pole-arm two-handed, Og had the strength to wield it by himself. On the opposite side of the waist was a mace, this time ogre-sized, that was Dog's weapon of choice.

As they walked, or as Grim walked, depending on how you choose to see it, both Og's and Dog's heads were covered in hemp sacks. To the extremely casual observer it looked like Grim had very large shoulders. By experience, they had found this was the best method of travelling. An ogre walking through human territory might often be the target of aggression. An ogre armed with pike and mace was generally left alone, in the hope that he was just passing through. An ogre with three heads, however, was almost always greeted with fear and hysteria. Treated as demon spawn or some such, the entire community would come together to exterminate it, perhaps in the belief they were doing their god's work.

Whatever the reason, Og-Grim-Dog had learned, by experience, to travel with the sacks. Since Grim did the walking, it didn't matter that the other two couldn't see. It also had the added benefit of muffling his brother's voices, thereby giving his ears a rest.

After walking across country for two days, Grim took them onto the road that led to the human settlement of Mer Khazer. No-one had tried to stop their passage—after all, they were just passing through. Grim decided it was safe enough from this point. Mer Khazer was a cosmopolitan town, attracting visitors from across the human lands and beyond. Three-headed ogres would always be on the edge of what was socially acceptable. But Grim judged that in Mer Khazer, they would get away with it.

'You can take the sacks off now.'

Dog ripped his off, gulping in air. All that Grim could hear from the other side was a gentle snoring.

'Og! We're on the road to Mer Khazer!'

Og woke with a start.

'I'm blind!' he moaned, before remembering what was happening. He took his sack off, a flustered look on his face. 'Where are we?'

'We're on the road to Mer Khazer,' Grim repeated, keeping the pace up. If he kept at it, they'd reach it by evening.

'Mer Khazer? Where's that?'

'You know Mer Khazer, Og,' Grim said patiently. 'We've been there several times.'

'Well, I don't recall it. What's the plan when we get there?'

'The trespassers meet in the inns of the town. We'll go to one of them and try to find out why they keep attacking our dungeon.'

'How about The Bruised Bollocks?' suggested Dog, sounding enthusiastic. 'They do a good quart of ale at The Bollocks.'

'The Bruised Bollocks?' asked Og. 'I don't remember us ever drinking there.'

As the three-headed ogre passed through the gates into the town of Mer Khazer, night crept in with them. It brought a chill to the air outside and the breath from three ogre mouths could be seen by three pairs of ogre eyes. Like so many others intent on staying awake after dark, the ogre headed to one of the many drinking establishments located about the centre of town.

The Bruised Bollocks was alive with the heat from the fire; with the sweet smells of roasted meat and yeasty beer; with the talk of the townsfolk of Mer Khazer, and of visitors from out of town. Og-Grim-Dog ducked under the lintel and entered the tap room. An array of glances were shot their way, from horror to amusement and everything in between, but the ogre was used to such reactions and ignored them, making its way to the bar and locking eyes with the man who served there. Keen to fulfil the order and keep his limbs intact, the barman soon deposited two quarts of ale into two hands, each the size of his head.

The third—Grim's drink—was left on the bar. As usual, he had to wait his turn while the other two took long glugs, smacking their lips contentedly. It wasn't unusual, when they were deep in their cups, for Grim to get forgotten about altogether. But this time, and without reminding, Og slammed his own drink back onto the bar and lifted Grim's to his lips for him. It had a nutty aroma and a bitter taste, and was the best thing Grim had tasted in months. Satisfied, Og-Grim-Dog put their back to the bar and took in the room.

It didn't take long to work out who was who. The townsfolk seemed naturally to congregate on one side of the room, and the foreigners on the other. It was the latter group that was of interest to Og-Grim-Dog. These were the trespassers: men and women who invaded and looted the dungeons of Gal'azu for profit. Warriors carried their weapons; wizards could be identified by their cloaks, hats or staves. Thieves, assassins and other rogues skulked about in dark corners; clerics wore the vestments of their holy orders, or carried the relics and trinkets of their gods on chains about their necks. It was an industry, a way of life, that attracted people from across Gal'azu, and even beyond. For the ogre could see other folk, too. Dwarves—short, stocky and bearded; elves—slim, with pointed ears and almond-shaped eyes; and there were other races—those allowed into human towns.

'No green-skins,' Dog muttered under his breath.

Grim began to mix amongst the trespassers, looking for a suitable group to talk with. Near the bar a group of young men spoke with the noise of those who had been drinking awhile. They were boasting, as young men do, of the creatures they had killed and the treasure they had won.

Killing goblins or orcs wasn't a boast amongst this crew. It had to be a dead troll; dead fimir; dead ogre. Grim could feel the animosity of his brothers grow; were these humans too far gone to notice a three-headed ogre standing behind them? Still, such talk wasn't new to Og-Grim-Dog. His brothers would control their anger. Wouldn't they?

'Next time we go dungeoneering, we need to step it up to the next level,' one of them suggested, leaving a dramatic pause to encourage the others in his party to listen. 'Next time, we find and kill a dragon.'

There was much agreement to this idea. In the comfort of an inn, miles from the nearest giant winged lizard, it's an easy enough thing to agree to.

Dog, however, wasn't impressed.

'Where does this obsession with finding dragons in dungeons come from?' he demanded, loud enough to attract the attention of the group, and many others in The Bruised Bollocks besides. 'Think about it. What are the two defining characteristics of a dragon? One, they can fly. Two, they are extremely large. Why, then, would they choose to confine themselves in an underground dungeon? I have been to the high mountain kingdoms of Old Nahru, trekked through the Inky Caverns of the Lost Ones. But I have never come across, nor ever heard of, an actual dragon in a dungeon. Yet the bizarre association remains.'

Many at The Bruised Bollocks stared open-mouthed at Dog's outburst. It was as if being lectured on dragons by a three-headed ogre was a new experience.

But one customer behaved differently. She was a powerful-looking warrior, perhaps from one of the barbarian tribes who inhabited the plains to the south. She looked Og-Grim-Dog firmly in the eye, not remotely intimidated.

'Come with me,' she suggested. 'I have a proposal for you.'

Not waiting for a response, she turned around and made her way to the back of the room. Grim followed her, squeezing through the throng of trespassers who cast bemused looks his way. The warrior offered him a wooden bench at a table. Grim sat down, and the warrior joined him. Two others sat at the table with them.

'I am Assata,' she said, offering her hand.

Dog grasped it in a handshake, her hand disappearing inside his. 'I am Dog. My brothers are Og and Grim.'

'This is Raya,' said Assata, introducing an elven woman at the table.

'Hi!' said the elf, raising one hand and giving a nervous, but friendly, smile.

'And Sandon.'

Sandon had the slim build and rune-inscribed robes that marked him out as a wizard. His looks were a curious mix of young and old, suggesting he was either prematurely aged or concealing his real looks. The wizard frowned at Og-Grim-Dog and placed a hand to his forehead.

'I sense you have come here with questions,' he said, a little too dramatically for Grim's taste. He'd sensed right, but Og-Grim-Dog were not about to reveal their mission to a stranger they had no reason to trust.

'We are putting together a team of adventurers,' Assata said.

Adventurers, Grim thought to himself. That was what the trespassers called themselves. Funny how one word can change the feel of a sentence; change one's view of the world, and one's place in it.

'If it works out, we could hit all the dungeons in the area. We've nearly filled all positions. But we could do with the extra muscle that you offer.'

Grim nodded. Judging by the present company, they were a bit lacking in the fighter department. Sandon brought the magic. Raya, he presumed, would offer ranged combat. And while Assata looked like she could handle herself in the melee, any group entering a dungeon needed more than one warrior to deal with the brutal savagery of close combat.

'We're interested,' Grim said. This sounded like the perfect way to find out why the trespassers were repeatedly targeting Darkspike Dungeon. *Infiltrate the enemy and learn their secrets*, he told himself, quite excited at the idea.

'Good. I'll introduce you to the other two members of the party as soon as I can,' said Assata, relaxing enough to give a tight smile.

With that, the real drinking began. The night followed the usual pattern. Og ended up falling asleep, snoring into Grim's left ear. Dog dominated the conversation at the table with his tales of all the famous people he had met; mostly made up. Grim's drink was left untouched.

He wasn't the only sober one, though. Sandon, to be fair, joined in, but he wasn't a big drinker. Assata had some concoction that she explained was alcohol-free. Grim had never heard of such a thing. When he asked her what was in it, she reeled off a load of mumbo jumbo, full of strange words like plant proteins, natural oils, glycogen replenishment and ergogenic ingredients. Raya had the same thing. But when she 'accidentally' picked up and necked Grim's drink, for the fifth time, he began to doubt her commitment to it.

Finally, when Dog started calling everyone 'darling', and 'treasure', Grim decided enough was enough. He got to his feet and took them off to bed.

THE BUREAU OF DUNGEONEERING

In the morning, they gathered in the courtyard of The Bruised Bollocks. There were six of them. Assata introduced Og-Grim-Dog to the final two members of their party of adventurers.

The first was a dwarf by the name of Gurin. He was an exceptionally grumpy looking individual, of an exceptionally grumpy race. He looked old in years—past his best, even. But dwarves were exceptionally good at locating and disabling traps; had a nose for finding their way when underground; and, judging by the mean looking axe strapped to his back, this one could fight, too.

'You've recruited an ogre?' Gurin asked, an incredulous tone to his voice, as he stared up balefully at Og-Grim-Dog. 'Ogres now go adventuring, do they? Another nail in the coffin of all that used to be sacred about this once great profession. I am just thankful that the great adventurers of the past— Larik the Bludgeoner, Randall the Heavy-Handed, to name but two—aren't alive now to see where it's all ended.'

'Nice to meet you, too,' said Og, rather sarcastically.

Dog just grunted, hungover from the night before, his breath smelling like he had eaten a cadaver for breakfast.

The second adventurer was quite different. Brother Kane was a baby-faced cleric with a beatific smile. He went out of his way to be friendly, insisting on giving each ogre brother a blessing. It involved ridiculous hand gestures, murmuring in a made-up language and being flicked in the face with water.

It wasn't easy for Grim to decide which of the two he disliked the most, so he resolved to hold off his final verdict until later.

'Well,' said Sandon, once the vial of holy water had been stoppered and tucked away. 'We really should make for the Bureau of Dungeoneering. There's a hell of a lot of red tape to get through these days,' he said apologetically.

Gurin the dwarf groaned, the sound of a tortured soul.

'Red tape?' Grim asked, as the wizard led them out of the courtyard and into one of the main streets of Mer Khazer. The centre of town was already busy, shops and stalls open for business, people buying and bartering, shouting and selling. All the incessant noise and activity of a human settlement—the frenetic pace, the restless need to be constantly doing something, that had seen humankind spread all over Gal'azu, establishing themselves as the dominant race.

'Paperwork,' Sandon explained. 'You can't go dungeoneering unless you're in a party that's been officially licensed. There are rules you must sign up to, health and safety checks to do. It *is* a bit of a pain, I must admit.'

Gurin spat. 'The hot shame of it—the betrayal of every ideal our fraternity ever held dear. Once we would raid here, sack there, on a whim. That was real freedom. The freedom to go wherever you liked, kill whatever creature that came to mind that particular day. Now, we have to ask permission from a bunch of pencil pushers who've never held a weapon themselves; never crawled on their hands and knees through the muck of a dungeon corridor, knowing that at any second you could trigger a spear trap and it's all over.'

'Hmm,' said Sandon. 'Though it was actually the adventurer community themselves who established the Bureau. The trouble was, all that freedom, combined with the growth in popularity of the movement, meant that dungeons were being explored so frequently that they didn't have time to restore themselves. The dungeon dwellers were close to extinction, their treasures looted; magic amulets and weapons all taken. We needed some way to keep them sustainable, or by now there would have been nothing left.'

Gurin harrumphed, but Grim found himself nodding along in agreement with the wizard. He remembered those days. 'But why are the dungeons being attacked so frequently again? Like they were before?'

Sandon gave him a frown. 'They're not. The Bureau's monitoring apparatus is more sophisticated now than it's ever been. Here we are.'

The Bureau of Dungeoneering was an unassuming office, nestled between a branch of Discount Dungeon Supplies and an imposing Gothic building with signage that identified it as Nick Romancer's Funeral Parlour. Inside, it was an open plan office that stretched farther back than Grim had imagined. Filing cabinets lined the walls. Several desks were staffed, paper racks full of forms sitting on top of them. Each desk was identified by a wooden nameplate: Registration; Magical Goods Declaration; Applications for Dungeon Crawls; Records; Financials; Human Resources; Non-Human Resources; Appeals, and so on.

They approached the desk marked Registration. A tall, willowy woman regarded them stern-faced from her little kingdom of paper, ink and rules. The thought of navigating the registration process filled Grim with a peculiar kind of dread, and he experienced a strange kind of relief when it was ended before it had begun.

'I'm sorry,' said the woman, not sounding very sorry at all. 'Your kind can't register,' she declared, pointing a long finger at Og-Grim-Dog.

'Why not?' demanded Og.

'Because you're an ogre,' she explained, a sour look on her face as if she had just been fed goblin dung. 'There are rules here, you know.'

'That's discrimination!' shouted Og. 'You can't do that!'

'Whoa, let's calm down,' intervened Assata with a look to Grim. 'I'm sure we can sort this out.'

'Yes, settle down Og,' Grim said to him quietly, so that no-one else could hear. 'Remember why we're here, after all. We need to find out how the system works. Let our new friends deal with it and we will observe the process.'

Grim turned to speak to Dog who looked at him with puffy eyes.

'When are we getting food?' Dog grumbled.

'Wait a little while longer,' Grim pleaded.

'Now,' Assata was saying to the woman, a fixed smile on her face. 'The five of us have registered individually. We just need to add Og-Grim-Dog and register as a party of six. We all vouch for him and are prepared to work with him. I agree to be held personally liable for any damage he does. But I assure you, there won't be any.'

The woman looked down her nose at Assata in much the same way as she had looked at Og-Grim-Dog. 'It's not a question of vouching or promises. It's the rules. And he is not allowed.'

'That's discrimination!' Assata shouted at the woman.

Raya led Assata away and Sandon replaced her in front of the desk.

'Now, now,' said the wizard. 'You say it is the rules and we understand that. Might I see the rules?'

'You can,' the woman said, sounding a little more reasonable. She pointed across the room. 'If you go to Records, they can provide a copy for you to peruse.'

Sandon raised his eyebrows at the rest of them and made for the Records desk.

'I've had enough of this nonsense,' growled Gurin, and grabbed Og's arm. He guided Og-Grim-Dog towards yet another desk: Non-Human Resources (NHR). 'Raya!' he called, and the elf dutifully came with them.

They found Non-Human Resources unstaffed. Gurin tapped the bell on the desk repeatedly, making a tinny ringing sound that eventually attracted someone.

'Oh, great,' Gurin said in a sarcastic voice as the member of staff approached. 'A centaur.'

'That's bad?' Grim asked.

'Centaurs are just about the most useless of creatures you could ever meet,' said the dwarf.

Raya gave Grim an apologetic little smile.

The centaur clopped up to the desk with his four horse legs. His top half was human, as naked as the rest of him, with a muscled torso and arms.

'Can I help?'

Gurin sighed. 'Let's hope so. My friend here has just been denied registration with the Bureau. This is exactly the kind of thing Non-Human Resources should be all over. It's blatant discrimination.'

'Hmm,' said the centaur, looking Og-Grim-Dog up and down. 'Ogre?'

'Of course he's an ogre,' said Gurin irritably.

'I don't recall an ogre ever being on our books, to be honest, but I can check. Two seconds,' he advised, and trotted over to one of the filing cabinets, where he pulled open one of the drawers and began flicking through the files therein.

Grim turned his neck to look over at Records. Sandon, Assata and Brother Kane were waiting there, presumably for someone to appear with a copy of the registration rules.

The centaur from Non-Human Resources (NHR) returned to the desk.

'I'm so sorry, we've never had an ogre on our books before. We once had a giant, if that's any help,' he said.

A wet sounding thud on the floor of the office could be heard after this statement.

'Did you just crap on the floor?' Gurin asked him.

The centaur turned around to look, revealing a pile of horse dung.

'Oh yes, so I did. Don't worry, I'll get that cleaned up in a minute.'

'That's pretty disgusting,' said Gurin.

'The thing is,' Raya piped up, 'we were really hoping that Non-Human Resources would represent our friend here. You know, demand he be allowed to register?'

'Ah, I see. Unfortunately, that's not the kind of thing we do. We represent all non-human adventurers who have been registered. If you have a query about Registration, you need to take it up with the Registration desk.'

'We've just come from there,' said the elf through gritted teeth. 'They said he can't register.'

'Right. Well, I'm not sure what the rules are to be honest. Can I suggest asking to see a copy from Records?'

'Brilliant,' said the elf. 'Thanks for your help.'

'You're welcome.'

They left for the Records desk. As they arrived, a member of staff arrived with a rolled-up piece of parchment and handed it over to Sandon. The wizard unrolled the scroll and placed it onto the desk. Og-Grim-Dog peered over the wizard's shoulder for a look.

'What does it say, Og?' Dog asked.

All Grim could see were endless horizontal lines in a minute scrawl. If there were letters and words in there, he couldn't make them out.

'I can't read that,' said Og, sounding equal parts irritated and offended.

Everyone else in their party looked and came away shaking their head or muttering darkly.

'Hmm,' said Sandon, somehow keeping a light tone to his voice. 'These rules seem to be a tad longer and more involved than I had anticipated. I suggest that Og-Grim-Dog and I pay a visit to my lawyer. If anyone can find a loophole, it's Mr Agassi.'

'Very well,' Assata agreed. 'The rest of us will get the provisions for the trip. We proceed on the basis that Og-Grim-Dog *is* coming with us.'

Everyone agreed. Grim found it touching that these people, whom he had only just met, were prepared to fight his corner rather than simply abandon him. It showed them in a very different light to the brutal murderers Queen Krim had described.

'Come on then, Og-Grim-Dog,' said Sandon. 'No time to waste.'

AN OGRE IN COURT

Sandon led Og-Grim-Dog towards what he called the Old Town. The earliest buildings of Mer Khazer were situated here, most notably the church, an attractive wooden structure surrounded by a graveyard. A tree-lined path separated the graveyard from a row of terraced houses, and it was to one of these houses that the wizard headed.

He knocked on the door. On the wall next to it was a small plaque that simply read *Agassi, Attorney at Law.* 'Oh, by the way,' he said, as they waited for the door to be opened, 'Mr Agassi is—'

The door opened. 'A ghoul,' said Mr Agassi.

Standing in the doorway was a rather startling figure. He was completely bald, making his head look like a skull. His ears stuck out, almost horizontally, and his eyes shone with a disturbing, green-tinged light. He was dressed very smartly, however, with a full suit and waistcoat, complete with silk tie and pocket square.

'There are some who don't like to be represented by a ghoul,' he said, looking at Og-Grim-Dog with his strange eyes.

'Well, given the nature of our business,' said Og, 'we can hardly object.'

Mr Agassi raised a hairless eyebrow at that, and then waved them into his small house. Og-Grim-Dog had to bend their body to get under the lintel. His front room was small and dark. Mr Agassi offered the ogre a rickety looking chair, but Og-Grim-

Dog decided it was safer to sit on the floor. The lawyer sat at his desk, while Sandon took the passed over chair.

'It's a dispute with the Bureau of Dungeoneering,' Sandon explained to Mr Agassi. 'They won't let Og-Grim-Dog register with them, on the basis that he's an ogre. We rather wanted him to join our party.'

'Discrimination!' declared Og.

Mr Agassi pursed his thin lips. 'The Bureau is a private organisation. There's nothing illegal about them discriminating in such a way. But there may be other avenues we could investigate.'

'Here,' said Sandon, producing the parchment he had been given at the Bureau. 'This is the constitution of the Bureau.'

Mr Agassi took the parchment and glanced at it. A little smile appeared on his face and his eyes lit up even brighter. 'It's always a good thing when a document is this long and complicated. More to work with. There's a good chance I could find something. But we need to discuss terms.'

'We don't have much in the way of valuables,' Grim said apologetically. 'I'm not sure we can afford lawyer's fees.'

Mr Agassi held his hand up. 'Nonsense. I know what it is like to live on the edges of human society. I will take this case on— no win, no fee. If I successfully get you registered with the Bureau, I will take a cut of any treasure your party wins. How about that?'

Og-Grim-Dog turned to look at Sandon.

'That sounds fair,' said the wizard.

'Excellent. I will peruse the document here and now. It shouldn't take me long. I have been doing this for a few hundred years, after all. But let me get you something to eat while you wait.'

Mr Agassi got to his feet and left the room.

'He's very good,' Sandon said reassuringly. 'I'm sure he'll find something.'

The ghoul soon returned with a meat platter, which he placed on his desk. 'Please, help yourselves.' He then settled back into his chair and began to study the document intensely, his spooky eyes poring over the words.

'Thanks be to Lord Vyana and His Horde of Winged Hyenas, I'm famished,' declared Dog. He grabbed a thick slab of juicy meat that made Grim's mouth water.

Sandon shook his head, his eyes wide. DON'T EAT THE MEAT, he silently mouthed.

Dog tore into the joint and began making satisfied noises as he chewed and swallowed.

'Oh, this is very good, Mr Agassi. What is it?'

'Hmm?' replied the ghoul, distracted from his reading. 'Oh, that. Just a little something I dug up.'

'Odd choice of words,' Dog murmured to Grim. 'Still, it's very good. Here, try some.'

※

Og-Grim-Dog stood, along with everyone else, as the District Judge of Mer Khazer entered the room. She motioned everyone to sit, and Og-Grim-Dog carefully settled into their chair, next to their lawyer, who gave them a reassuring pat on the leg.

He knew it was silly, but Grim felt nervous about being in court. He peered behind him to the rows of wooden seats. His new friends responded with a few winks and thumbs up. Assata raised one arm and made a fist. It made him feel better to know they had some support.

'We couldn't have done better than Judge Deborah,' Mr Agassi whispered. 'She's not long out of law school but she's already going places. Very fair. No nonsense.'

Indeed, the judge seemed keen to get on with things.

'The plaintiff?' she demanded, unable to hide a little look of surprise when she glanced at Og-Grim-Dog.

'I am representing Mr Og-Grim-Dog,' said Mr Agassi smoothly. 'We are arguing that he has been incorrectly denied registration with the Bureau of Dungeoneering. He is merely seeking this ban to be revoked.'

'Is it Mr or Messrs?' asked the judge.

'Ah, well, the strict identity of said ogre would be a far more convoluted issue to iron out, Your Honour, and with all due respect to the bench, might I suggest it is unnecessary for us to get stranded on those particular legal rocks when dealing with a simple case such as this?'

'Agreed,' said the judge. 'The defendant? You are challenging the claim, I presume, Mr Sampras?'

Defending for the Bureau of Dungeoneering was a tall man of middle to late years who looked like he had been born in a suit. He was giving off a bit of lawyerly attitude, as if he was already bored of being here.

'The constitution of the Bureau of Dungeoneering outlines its rules of membership. With respect, Your Honour, they are a private association, entitled to pass whatever membership rules they wish.'

'Your Honour,' said Mr Agassi. 'We are contending that said rules were not properly applied.'

'Then this court simply has to decide whether the rules were fairly implemented?' asked the judge.

Both lawyers nodded their agreement.

The judge gave a sigh of relief. 'Then let's get this over with, gentlemen. There are other matters for this court to attend to, after all.'

'May I get to the point directly?' asked Mr Agassi. 'I have read this document from beginning to end and nowhere, at all, does it even mention the words ogre or ogres.'

Gasps could be heard around the court.

'Oh really, Agassi, that is quite misleading,' said Sampras from the Bureau in a disappointed tone. 'You must know that the rule of ejusdem generis applies here. Your Honour, may I read out loud the relevant passage?'

'I think that would be most useful,' said the judge.

'Section Four, sub-section two reads as follows. 'Goblins, orcs, trolls and other such monsters shall, under no condition, be admitted as members of the Bureau of Dungeoneering.' Now, since I know that Your Honour is very well versed in the law, may I explain this for the benefit of everyone else in court, including perhaps for my learned friend Mr Agassi?'

The judge nodded her consent. Mr Agassi's green-tinged eyes darkened with anger.

'The rule of ejusdem generis states that where general words follow specific words in a statutory enumeration, the general words are construed to embrace objects similar in nature to those objects enumerated by the preceding specific words. In other words, whilst sub-section two only mentions goblins, orcs and trolls by name, when it then goes on to say 'other such monsters' it is, quite clearly, meant to also include ogres.'

Og and Dog turned to Grim at the exact same moment, confused and upset expressions on their faces.

'What is happening?' Dog whispered.

Grim didn't know what was happening. 'Let's just trust Mr Agassi, shall we?'

'Where we disagree, sir,' said Mr Agassi sharply, 'is your presumption that ogres are to be included under the term 'other such monsters'. We contend that ogres are in fact not so similar in nature to goblins, orcs and trolls as to fall under sub-section two, and therefore my client should not have been excluded from membership of the Bureau.'

'So, if I have it correct,' said the judge, 'the disagreement is not on the application of ejusdem generis itself, but whether or not ogres are sufficiently similar to the three creatures listed as to fall under the rule?'

'Precisely, Your Honour,' said Mr Agassi.

Sampras representing the Bureau shrugged his acceptance. 'Yes, but surely that is not a matter for debate?'

'I will hear arguments,' said the judge.

'Will the creature take the stand?' asked Sampras.

Mr Agassi turned to Og-Grim-Dog. 'Now, remember I said you might be asked some questions? Now is that time. Just answer truthfully. No cleverness.'

Grim nodded. He really didn't think they had it in them to be clever.

'Mr Og-Grim-Dog will take the stand,' said the ghoul.

Grim stood and walked over to a little box next to the judge, which Mr Agassi had called the witness stand. It was a bit of a squeeze to get into, but he made it. From this position he was the same height as the judge, and could see over the heads of all those who had come to court.

'Your witness, Mr Sampras,' said Judge Deborah.

The lawyer from the Bureau gave a little sigh, as if this was all too silly. It *was* a bit silly, Grim thought. But then why wouldn't the Bureau just back down?

'Now, Mr Og-Grim-Dog, I understand that the word 'monster' can sound pejorative; can be hurtful. So, let me ask you some simple questions. Have you ever killed a human?'

'Of course,' said Dog, a little more casually than Grim would have said it. 'But humans kill each other, no?'

Mr Sampras smiled. 'Indeed. Have you ever…eaten a human?'

'Yes,' said Dog, as if the answer were obvious.

Gasps rang around the courtroom.

Mr Sampras's smile grew a little wider. 'Now, can you tell me where you live? Where your home is?'

'Darkspike Dungeon,' said Og.

'And what other creatures live in Darkspike Dungeon?'

'Well, there are kobolds upstairs from us. And then there are goblins, orcs, trolls—'

Grim winced. The courtroom muttered. This didn't seem to be going well.

'Objection!' Mr Agassi interrupted. 'This is establishing guilt by association.'

'Mr Agassi,' said the judge sharply. 'This is not a criminal trial and so the concept of guilt has no place. Further, establishing association is at the heart of the matter in question. Continue, Mr Sampras.'

'No further questions, Your Honour.'

'Your witness, Mr Agassi.'

Mr Agassi replaced Mr Sampras in front of the witness stand.

'Og-Grim-Dog, you live with these creatures and must know more about them than anyone else here. I wish to find out more about them. Firstly, what colour is their skin?'

'Objection!' snapped Mr Sampras. 'Your Honour, surely this is more than a question of skin colour?'

'Mr Agassi?'

'Of course it is, Your Honour. I'm just laying the groundwork.'

'Mr Agassi, I expect you to complete the groundwork with speed and move on to constructing the building.'

'Of course, Your Honour. Og-Grim-Dog?'

'They're greenskins,' said Dog.

'Stay quiet, Og,' Grim whispered as his other brother stirred at the use of this term. 'Now's not the time.'

Og let out a small harrumph but otherwise kept his peace.

'Ah. Greenskins is a term you use for these creatures?'

'Yes,' answered Dog.

'And ogres aren't greenskins?'

'Of course not!'

'These races, whom you collectively call greenskins, they live together in large numbers?'

'Yes, they live together in tribes.'

'And ogres?'

'We live alone.'

'Ah. Another difference,' commented Mr Agassi.

'Oh, come on!' blurted out Mr Sampras. 'How can you say they live alone when there's three of them!'

Mr Agassi made a rather smarmy face at the judge. 'Your Honour, we did agree we weren't going to go there.'

'We did, Mr Agassi. Continue.'

'Now, Og-Grim-Dog, you travelled from your dungeon to Mer Khazer. Where did you go when you arrived here?'

'The Bruised Bollocks.'

'The Bruised Bollocks. Did you see any goblins, orcs or trolls in The Bollocks?'

'No.'

'I don't think they would be allowed in, do you?'

'Definitely not.'

'But you were?'

'Yes.'

'And at The Bollocks, you met a group of adventurers who asked you to join their dungeoneering party?'

'Yes.'

'I think it highly unlikely that they would have asked a goblin, or an orc, to join them. Don't you?'

'Very highly unlikely.'

'One final question. In your travels, have you ever seen a goblin, or an orc, or a troll, with more than one head?'

'Never.'

'Thank you, Og-Grim-Dog. You may return to your seat now.'

Once Grim returned to their seat, the judge seemed eager to get to her decision, asking the two lawyers to keep their summaries brief.

'Your Honour,' said Mr Sampras. 'This creature has admitted to being a man-eating monster. The rules drawn up by the Bureau were clearly designed to prevent such monsters from becoming members. A common-sense verdict would see this ogre barred from membership.'

'Mercifully brief, Mr Sampras. Thank you. Mr Agassi?'

'Your Honour, this decision rests on the rule of ejusdem generis. How similar are ogres to goblins, orcs and trolls? I have established that in some key respects, they are quite different. Is there some doubt, therefore, about the membership rules of the

Bureau? I believe there is. Now, if Mr Sampras and the Bureau wish to go off and rewrite their constitution to add ogres to their list, and they make such an amendment according to the rules of their organisation, they have the right to do so. But as things stand, there is sufficient doubt on the question for me to suggest that the Bureau has been over hasty and unfair in its handling of my client's case. I would hope, therefore, that the court would come down on the side of the individual over the organisation.'

'Agreed,' said the judge. 'It is far from clear to me that Mr Og-Grim-Dog is banned from membership of the Bureau of Dungeoneering. I therefore rule that he has a right to registration. Thank you, everyone.'

The judge got to her feet, and everyone else in the room did the same. Once she left, there was a little cheer from Assata, Sandon and the others from the benches behind them. Agassi and Sampras shook hands, seemingly friendly enough.

'Congratulations, Agassi,' said Sampras. 'And to you, Og-Grim-Dog. Happy adventuring.'

He offered his hand and Og took it in his.

'Did we win then?' Dog asked.

'We did,' said Mr Agassi. 'I suggest you head over to the Bureau this very instant and get your name on the register. Before that constitution is changed.'

FORM ADC6

The elation of the court victory was short-lived for Og-Grim-Dog, since it meant a return to the offices of the Bureau of Dungeoneering.

There were forms to be filled in at the Registration desk, and then follow up forms at NHR. Once Og-Grim-Dog had become a fully-fledged member of the Bureau, they and their new friends had to present themselves at the Applications for Dungeon Crawls desk.

The clerk at the desk needed to give the party approval for each dungeon they wished to visit. Those that had been visited too frequently in recent weeks were forbidden to them. A lively conversation ensued over where they should go, this or that dungeon, and the best route to take. The clerk's advice was soon ignored, as Gurin tried to dominate the decision-making process with reference to his vast experience; Assata stood firm against him; and Sandon took the role of sensible peacekeeper. Brother Kane smiled beatifically throughout, while Raya rolled her eyes at Og-Grim-Dog when she was sure no-one else was looking.

The clerk looked more than a little relieved when they had settled on a plan. It involved hitting six dungeons in a ten-day period, with the promise of significant opportunities for loot.

'One final thing,' he said, yet another form clutched in his tiny human hands. 'Form ADC6. A new directive from the Bureau.

We now need to record surnames and I must record a name for your party.'

A barrage of complaints hit him at this new imposition.

'What if we don't have surnames?' Gurin demanded. 'None of the best dungeon crawlers had surnames. Reginald Shit-Blood didn't have a surname, did he?'

'We will accept nicknames,' said the clerk, which seemed to mollify things a little. He put his piece of paper onto the desk in front of him and handed a quill to Brother Kane, perhaps with the idea that he was the least likely to snap it in two.

In the left-hand column, the cleric wrote **Brother**, and in the right-hand column **Kane**.

With a long-suffering look, the clerk invited Sandon next.

Sandon Branderson

Everyone gave the wizard a silent look.

'Are you for real?' Assata asked him.

'What?' he demanded.

'Never mind. Hand me the quill. No-one gets to know my surname,' she said.

Assata S

RAYA SUNSHINE

'My parents were hippies,' said the elf apologetically. 'Do you have a surname, Og-Grim-Dog?'

'Hmm,' pondered Og. 'We have three names. Maybe we could put Dog as the surname?'

'We're not putting Dog as the surname,' Dog retorted, though Grim wasn't convinced Dog knew what he was objecting to. 'Dog is *my* name.'

'Well, what do people call you?' Raya asked them kindly.

'Oh, I see,' said Og, carefully taking the quill in his huge hand.

Og Grim Dog. The Three Headed Ogre.

Og passed the quill down to the dwarf, who muttered darkly to himself before scrawling down his name.

Gurin Fuckaxe

'What in hell?' said Assata, shocked. 'Fuckaxe? That's just wrong, man. That's dirty.'

'Eh?' said Gurin, bristling. 'Not in that kind of way. I didn't mean it like that. I mean I fuck people up. With my axe.'

'I'm really not sure you want that as your surname,' said Raya in a concerned voice. 'It just sounds indecent.'

The dwarf threw his hands in the air. 'It's done now, isn't it? I've already written it.'

'You could cross it out?' Sandon suggested.

'Well, I like it,' said Dog. '"Fuck with me, and you get the axe."' He barked with laughter.

'See, he gets it,' said Gurin, stabbing his thumb at Dog. 'Come on, let's get out of here. I'm not wasting any more time on this nonsense.'

'I still need a name for your party?' the clerk dared to ask.

'We're called Team Shove It Up Your Ass,' said Gurin.

They left the Applications for Dungeon Crawls desk, leaving behind a clerk clutching Form ADC6, a pitiful expression on his face.

*

The party of six were ready to go bright and early the next morning. All legal boxes had been ticked; all provisions bought and packed away in knapsacks. They strode through the streets of Mer Khazer and the people of the city applauded them. Sellers shouted out encouragement as they got their stalls ready for business. People on their way to work gave advice about where exactly Assata should stick her sword, or Og his pike.

It wasn't just that Mer Khazer was an adventurer's town—had been for years—and was therefore sympathetic to parties of adventurers. It was also that dungeoneers kept down the local populations of monsters, and the citizens were grateful for it. Last night, The Bollocks had been full of stories of orc bands roaming the countryside, causing mayhem. Such stories didn't chime in with what Queen Krim had told them. Og-Grim-Dog would have to keep their eyes peeled if they were to learn the truth about what was going on.

But such thoughts were at the back of the ogre's minds. Right now, they were experiencing a strange sensation.

'Grim,' said Og, putting a hand to his chest. 'I have a warm feeling here.'

'Me too.'

Literally, the same place. It wasn't the first time that Grim suspected he shared a heart with his brother.

'Are we heroes?' asked Dog.

'Maybe,' said Grim. 'Or perhaps we will be when we come back victorious. It's a nice feeling, isn't it?'

'It sure is,' said Og. 'I can understand the attraction of adventuring now. Don't get me wrong, staying underground in our cavern is good, too. But this is more—I don't know.'

'Fulfilling?' Grim asked.

'Yes,' Og agreed. 'That's a good word for it.'

They left via the city gates and took the road north. Grim had been doubtful that all his companions would be able to walk at a decent pace, but he was proved wrong.

Assata and Gurin marched at the front, both seemingly under the impression that they were the one in charge. Raya walked some feet behind the rest of the group. At first, Grim took this for dawdling, but after a while he saw that she would take glances behind them, or veer away from the road a little way to stand atop a rise or hillock and look about.

'Why is she doing that?' Dog asked when he noticed her walking to a mound in the distance.

'Elves are only small,' Grim conjectured, 'and therefore have many predators. I expect this is something they do to keep safe.'

'Oh, it's an elf thing,' said Dog, a little dismissively.

'Actually,' said the wizard Sandon, overhearing the conversation, 'Raya is one of the most respected adventurers of her generation. Her caution and care has got me through many a scrape, I can tell you.'

'How long have you been doing this?' Grim asked him.

'Oh, for years. Before the Bureau even existed.'

✽

After a bit of squabbling, Assata and Gurin agreed to leave the road and cut across country towards the first dungeon on their list. For the first couple of miles they walked through farmland and past small settlements, that clung tightly to the safety of the road. But beyond this thin zone of human habitation was wild, untamed land, that you didn't enter without the numbers and weapons to back you up.

'Deepwood Dungeon is in the heart of the forest,' the barbarian explained, pointing into the distance to a treeline that was the beginning of the woodland. 'It's one of the closest dungeons to Mer Khazer, but most parties avoid it because you have to get through the woods to reach it. It's not even worth considering unless you have an elven guide with you. Luckily for us, we have the best in the business.'

Raya gave a self-conscious little salute.

They made their camp amongst the trees that evening. It wasn't an environment much suited to ogres: the wood was a maze full of snags to trip you up and the game was small and agile. Og-Grim-Dog contented themselves with collecting wood, which Gurin turned into a blazing fire. Sandon and Brother Kane fetched water from a brook and the dwarf soon had a pot bubbling. Assata appeared with a brace of rabbits and she and Gurin paunched the animals with practised ease.

'Good source of protein,' commented the barbarian. 'Just not much of it.'

Finally, Raya appeared. She had filled her knapsack with vegetables and herbs. She emptied it onto the ground for everyone to inspect. Most plentiful were long, greenish-yellow sticks that the elf called 'carrots'. Grim thought they looked revolting, but even Dog had the manners not to openly complain about the elf's efforts.

'Oh, you found mushrooms?' Assata asked, an excited tone to her voice. 'Full of antioxidants, you know.'

'Maybe we should throw them out, then?' Dog suggested.

Assata laughed. 'You are funny, Dog.'

'I wasn't joking,' Dog mumbled under his breath, until Grim hushed him.

'I haven't seen ones that look like that before,' Assata added.

'Erm—yes, well, these ones tend to only grow in the Deepwood,' said Raya.

'Oh. We're lucky to have you with us,' said Assata. 'We've got some rabbit. Any suggestions?'

'The simplest way to cook rabbit well is to drown it with booze,' said Raya.

'Oh,' said the barbarian, looking disappointed. 'That's so unhealthy. We've done so well with our abstinence as well, Raya.'

'I know, it's a shame,' said the elf, who didn't sound very disappointed to Grim's ears. 'But think how healthy the rest of the meal is.'

'I suppose.'

And so the rabbit went in the pot with the carrots and the other vegetables, and the herbs and mushrooms as well, along with a generous helping of Kuthenian red wine. When it was served, even Dog had to admit it was a tasty stew.

From then on, Grim's memory of the night was somewhat hazy.

Afterwards, everyone agreed that it was just as well that they had the elf with them. For the Deepwood was full of strange sights and sounds that night.

Sandon swore that the Queen of the Fairies had appeared and tried to lead him off through the trees to her realm. Fortunately, he was saved when he tripped over a tree root and knocked himself unconscious.

Assata said she had fought against foul winged demons, killing at least six of the creatures. There was no sign of their bodies the next morning, though Raya mentioned that demon corpses did have a tendency to melt away into a fine mist.

Gurin had apparently been visited by his ancestors, who had told him many ancient secrets of his race. Come morning, he struggled to remember them, except that his great-grandfather, Cracked Blurin, had in fact been a Merman disguised as a dwarf. Gurin insisted that this fact explained a lot, though Grim remained rather doubtful.

As for Og-Grim-Dog, they had come under attack from a giant spider. Grim distinctly remembered that Dog had seen it first, and he heard his own voice trying to reassure his brother that the spider wasn't actually that large. Then Raya had said 'how about now?' and suddenly he had come face to face with its huge eyes and had screamed in terror.

Everyone agreed that while all these disturbing encounters had been taking place, an unceasing maniacal laughter had echoed throughout the forest. The more Grim thought about it, the more he thought it had sounded like Brother Kane, which made it all the more bizarre and terrifying.

It was only in the morning of the next day that their sanity returned. Grim slowly woke from a daze to find himself walking through the forest. Og and Dog were both clutching a length of rope and when Grim looked about he saw that everyone in their party had a grip of the same rope. Ahead, Raya had the rope tied about her middle and was leading them along a path that cut through the dense trees of the Deepwood.

When she heard the mumbles and muttering of her friends waking from their stupor, she stopped, and let them catch up to her. 'We made it through the worst terrors that the Deepwood could throw at us,' she told them. 'Well done, everyone. This path takes us to the dungeon. We're nearly there.'

DEEPWOOD DUNGEON: LEVEL ONE

The path ended in front of a cream-coloured building made from giant slabs of marble. Balusters rose up the length of the walls, while green moss and the climbing plants of the Deepwood had made the exterior their home.

Grim's eyes were drawn to the archway that led inside the building. Beyond it was shadow, somehow both inviting and foreboding at the same time. Sitting just above the archway was a peaked marble roof and either side of it two decorative pillars. When Grim looked closer, he saw that what he had taken for pillars were actually marble statues, both of them worn and chipped. But he could clearly see that they were hooded figures, with both hands on the hilt of a sword that ran vertically down, so that the point of the blade was inches above the ground.

'Deepwood Dungeon,' said Gurin with some reverence. 'A fitting challenge for our first dungeon crawl together.'

Without being told to, everyone in the party made last minute adjustments to their packs and armour. Weapons that had been carried on backs or at belts were now in hands. Tension gripped Grim's belly. Once they passed under that archway, they had to be ready.

They looked at one another for a few seconds more. They all knew that they would have to work as a team; rely on each other to survive. It was good to look your friends in the eye before you stepped into Gehenna.

'Let's do this,' said Assata. Her voice was quiet but steady.

The barbarian went first, the dwarf at her shoulder. Og-Grim-Dog went third. These were the fighters of the group. Behind them, Sandon, Kane and Raya offered a different skill set.

Assata put one foot through the arch, legs bent and balanced, strong and supple.

'Steady now,' Gurin whispered. 'Let me have a look at what we have here.'

He inched past the barbarian and peered into the darkness. He waited a while. Gurin probably had the best eyes for seeing underground, but he still needed to let them adjust to the sudden lack of light. The others waited for him. Grim could see Dog's knuckles whiten as he gripped his mace hard, ready to react if needed.

'A corridor to the left and right,' whispered Gurin at last. 'Empty. Something odd looking to the left. I'm going to investigate. Wait here for me. I won't be long.'

The dwarf disappeared into the pitch black of the dungeon. They waited for him to return, the time dragging. Grim saw Raya look back into the forest behind them, her fingers on her bowstring, an anxious expression on her face.

Gurin's face reappeared at the archway.

'There's a pit trap to the left,' he said, pitching his voice just loud enough for everyone to hear. 'Quite elaborate looking. It would take a long time to dismantle. I presume its sole purpose is to catch out unwary adventurers, and that the denizens of the dungeon follow the corridor to the right. That means we can probably access the whole of the dungeon that way. Is everyone agreed?'

Everyone nodded. The layout Gurin described made sense to Grim. Multiple access points would simply make the dungeon more vulnerable. This way, trespassers would be funnelled in a single direction.

Tentatively, Assata and Gurin moved into the corridor and turned right. Grim followed them. The corridor was only just wide enough to comfortably walk down. Maybe that's a good thing, Grim told himself. It suggested that they wouldn't find anything much bigger than an ogre.

When they were all in the corridor they waited, trying to get used to the sudden lack of light. It was the only way to do it. Grim had witnessed first time trespassers trying to creep through a dungeon carrying torches. It never ended well for them. It wasn't just that the dungeon dwellers saw them coming. They heard them, too—coughing and spluttering from the fumes that the torches released in a closed space. It was one of the reasons dwarves and halflings and the like were so sought after in the world of adventuring. Their eyes were a match for most anyone, or anything.

Grim's weren't so bad either. He began to make out smoothly cut walls on each side. Above, the ceiling joined at a perfect right angle. Whoever had originally built this place, for whatever purpose, they had known what they were doing.

They began to move along the dark corridor. Ogres are physically unable to creep, or sneak, but Grim did his best to move quietly, aware that he was making much more noise than anyone else.

They came upon two wooden doors, directly opposite one another. Almost certainly guard rooms, typically full of the most expendable soldier in the dungeon.

Grim knew there were two main schools of thought when it came to guard rooms. Firstly, sneak past and head for the lower levels of the dungeon, where the valuable items would be stashed. This approach suited groups full of thieves and other rogues. Second option, charge in and neutralise them as quickly as possible, so that they don't get in your way when you're leaving the dungeon. This approach seemed to be much the better fit for their party.

Assata invited Og-Grim-Dog to the door on the left. Grim felt honoured. The barbarian stood ready with her sword on the far side of the door, the dwarf with his axe on the near side. The elf put an arrow to her bowstring. The cleric smiled, and the wizard nodded nervously.

Grim leaned back a little and then kicked at the door with the sole of his foot. He followed it into the room. Goblins. About ten of them. Grim didn't stop, instead moving towards the far end of the room, leaving space for the others to get into. As the goblins screamed their challenges and came for them, it was Og and Dog's turn to act. Og thrust his pike at the enemy, threatening to skewer them with the sharp spearhead. Dog waved his mace about, aiming to connect with a massive blow. He caught a goblin that got too close, sending it crashing to the floor.

It hadn't been easy for Og-Grim-Dog to learn how to fight: often, painfully frustrating. Coordinating movement and weapon striking between the three of them had taken years to perfect. Now, though, they were able to use their unique physique as an advantage. All Grim had to think about was movement. He kept his balance, kept his feet moving, turning this way and that. This made it very difficult for an opponent to sneak up from behind, since Og and Dog were looking out from both sides. All his brothers had to do was land an accurate hit. All they had to worry about was one arm and one weapon. Individually, there wasn't the kind of skill that would impress a weapons master. But together, they could be brutally effective.

Four goblins were trying to harry the ogre, staying out of range of Og's pike, looking for an opening where they could get past the defences and get a strike in. An arrow caught one of them in the chest, and Grim decided it was time to go on the offensive. He launched themselves towards one of the goblins, reducing the distance to allow Dog to reach it with his mace. Meanwhile, Og would be using his pike to keep the other two at bay. Dog's bark of triumph signalled success. Quickly, Grim moved for the next one. He saw Dog's mace come down on its head, turning it to a pulpy mess. The last goblin panicked, turning away and running. But it got too close to the barbarian, and Assata ran it through with her sword.

'Watch out!' cried Sandon, backing away from the door they had come through. More goblins poured into the room, no doubt arriving from the guardroom opposite this one, alerted by the noise of fighting. 'Don't worry,' he continued, 'I have just the spell. The witches of the ice realm of Fjordlund were the first to learn how to take the water from the air and turn it into ice. I will bring forth a wall of ice and encase the enemy inside!'

The wizard began his incantation.

Raya released an arrow, sending the nearest goblin to the floor.

'Come on!' shouted Dog, and Grim found himself charging at the goblins with a great roar. Assata came with him on one side and Gurin on the other, and the two forces crashed into one another.

Dog was especially fond of fighting and he began to bark loudly. It was a terrifying noise to the enemy, but few realised that he was actually laughing. Every time he hit a goblin, or a strike from Gurin's axe sprayed gore into his face, he found it all the more amusing, and the barking got louder.

Og, on the other hand, failed to take pleasure in combat—Grim had known him to simply stop without warning in the middle of a fight before, declaring himself bored. Fortunately, he didn't pull that this time, but his pike thrusts were beginning to look distinctly lacklustre. It was enough, though, since Assata fought by his side and was able to pick up the slack.

Grim watched as she demonstrated her skills. She moved with grace and power, each strike of her sword beginning with her powerful legs, strong enough to knock aside the swings of the enemy. At other times she let the goblins come to her, fooling them into thinking they had found a way through her defences, before a wristy twist of the hilt sent her blade towards them from an unexpected direction, faster than they had allowed for.

Despite having been outnumbered, they tore through the goblins until not one was left alive. Looking about the room, Grim thought at least twenty of the creatures lay dead.

Sandon stopped his incantation. 'Ah, well done everyone!' he enthused. 'You finished the job before I got a chance to get through my spell. Still, no matter, that means I still have all my energy for later. Some magic users call it mana, others power; but either way, my ability to use magic is limited and the more I cast, the less I can use until I have recovered. There are ways to boost mana—certain items, for example—'

Grim quickly stopped listening to the wizard's boring speech. How odd that he had decided to start talking like that. Elsewhere, Gurin had taken a seat on a table and was being tended to by Brother Kane. It looked like he had received a knock from a blunt weapon on the forearm. The cleric rubbed a salve into the affected area, muttering a prayer as he did so. Assata and Raya, meanwhile, were searching the room.

'You don't expect to find treasure here, do you?' Og asked them.

'Not treasure, no,' said Assata. 'But there may be other items of use.'

'Such as this,' said Raya, holding up a metal key she had found in a desk.

Grim did sometimes wonder why goblins had desks in their rooms. He had never, ever—not once—met one who could read, let alone write.

Raya's face fell somewhat. 'What are you doing?' she asked, looking at Dog.

Grim turned his head. Dog was munching on a goblin arm.

'Sorry,' Dog said, picking up from the look on the elf's face that he had done something wrong, even if he wasn't sure what it was. 'But fighting a pack of goblins is hungry work.'

Assata looked ready to be sick.

'Why are you eating that?' asked the barbarian. 'I packed your bag full of provisions.'

'And we ate those on the way.'

'Ate them all? They were meant to last you the whole trip!'

Three ogre heads focused on the barbarian. Dog barked with laughter. 'Ha-ha! Good one, Assata! Last us the whole trip, she says!'

DEEPWOOD DUNGEON: LEVEL TWO

They carried out a brief search of the second guardroom, but found nothing of interest, and everyone agreed that it was best to keep moving. They continued down the corridor in the same formation as before, Assata and Gurin leading the way. The adrenaline of battle still pumped around Og-Grim-Dog's body and it wasn't easy for Grim to revert to being stealthy. He did his best.

It wasn't far until the corridor came to an end at a set of marble steps. They spiralled down into a heavier darkness—an underground darkness. Grim could smell the dampness of the dungeon proper.

Forced into single file by the narrow steps, Gurin led them down. Og-Grim-Dog went third, behind Assata. At the back of the group was Raya, ready in case the denizens of the dungeon came at them through a secret door or similar ruse. All was quiet as they descended, however. It seemed that the commotion they had made in the guard rooms had not disturbed those that dwelled in the lower levels.

The stairs ended in an open area plenty large enough for them to gather together. Grim saw that this level was constructed from stone rather than marble. But it still bore the hallmarks of design rather than a natural space. The floor and the walls were smooth and followed straight lines. Two corridors ran off from the stairs, at right angles to one another. Peering as far as he could along each, Grim saw nothing that might indicate which was the better route.

Gurin held his arms up horizontally so that each followed one of the corridors.

'Assuming these continue to run straight,' he said, his voice so quiet that Grim had to strain to hear him, 'which it appears they do, they carve out a rectangular shape to this floor. I would guess that we want to head towards the centre of the rectangle.'

'So which way?' Grim asked.

The dwarf shrugged. He took a coin from his pocket.

'Heads left,' said Assata.

Gurin flipped the coin and slapped it down onto his hand. He squinted in the darkness. 'Right,' he said.

It was the right corridor they took. They crept along, and as they went, they heard noises echoing in the dungeon, their origin hard to place. Bangs and crashes and raised voices.

'Orcs,' Grim warned the others.

Doors appeared in both walls of the corridor ahead of them— some with light leaking through, others dark and ominous looking. If the plan was to head to the centre of this level, they should take one in the left-hand wall. But which? Gurin led them past the first. A thought crossed Grim's mind then, and he found it odd that it hadn't before. Had the dwarf been here before? The way Gurin talked, he had many years of adventuring behind him. Was it possible that he had never in all those years come to this dungeon? Even if it had been a long time ago, wouldn't he remember the basic layout?

The dwarf stopped next to one of the doors that had light behind it. He gestured at it, making a fist. The unmistakeable sound of orcs could be heard behind it. It was fighting time again.

Gurin gripped the handle and pushed. The door held firm. Locked.

Raya pushed her way to the door. She took the key she had found from her pocket and placed it into the keyhole. She twisted it and they all heard the unmistakeable click of the locking mechanism. Replacing the key, she took her bow in hand and fitted an arrow to it. She nodded to Assata.

The barbarian opened the door and Raya went through, drawing her bow. The others followed her in. The room looked like a typical living quarter for orcs: they slept and ate in the same place. There was a row of pallets on the floor and a cauldron simmered on top of a smoky fire. Two fat candles burned on the floor next to it. No orcs, though. On the other side of the room a door was wide open and Grim could see that it led out into a large space.

Just as he was looking in that direction, a single orc entered through the door. Perhaps she had come to tend the cauldron. The orc did a double take when it saw the trespassers in its room. Then, it collapsed to the floor with a thud, an elven arrow protruding from its head.

Everyone froze, sure that the noise would have been heard. But no shouts of alarm came. Tentatively, the group began to look about the room. Gurin made his way to the far door, carefully peering out. Grim approached the bubbling cauldron. Dog stirred the contents with a big metal serving spoon before withdrawing it. Politely, he let Og and Grim take a sip before bringing it to his own mouth. The soup tasted of the bones and fat of some creature, hard to say what.

'Not bad,' suggested Og.

Gurin waved them over. 'Not many creatures about,' he said. 'We may have struck lucky and come when the orcs of this dungeon are out raiding. That said, the stairs leading down to the next level are in the middle of this square,' he said, gesturing through the door at the large, open plaza, surrounded by stone-built rooms that opened onto it. 'Everything on this level will see us when we head for them.'

'Then perhaps now is my time to contribute,' said Sandon. 'In the deserts of Karak-Tar the mystics of the sand tribes developed a form of mind control that protected their people from the giant Slaath worms. They sent a signal from their minds that convinced the worms that all they saw was sand. A psychic camouflage, if you will. I studied in Karak-Tar for three years, learning their ways, perfecting their techniques; but not only that. I developed a method that would allow me to use this form of mind control on other creatures, in different environments. When I am done, we will be able to walk out of here to the stairs without being seen.'

'That sounds perfect, Sandon,' enthused Raya.

Sandon touched each side of his head with two fingers, dropped his chin to his chest, and closed his eyes.

'Dawada, afeaa,' he chanted. 'Dawada! Afeaa!' Louder now.

'What in Gehenna is that noise?' came a voice. An orc appeared at the doorway. 'Trespassers!' he got out, before Assata clobbered him across the head with her sword, sending him to the floor. But it was too late. Shouts began to erupt around the square.

'Come on,' said Gurin. 'We'll have to go.' He was the first through the door.

'Dawada?' Sandon uttered. Og put his hand around the wizard's arm and dragged him out of the room.

They ran for the centre of the square, where a set of stone steps led down. From all around the square, orcs appeared. They shouted; drew weapons; gave chase. Perhaps Gurin was correct, and many were out raiding. But there were still plenty of them. Grim knew they had to make it to the stairs before they were surrounded and overwhelmed. Dog squealed with delight at the chase, smashing away with his mace at any orc that got within range.

Grim made it to the steps. 'We'll keep them at bay,' he shouted, as Og encouraged Sandon to begin the descent. Gurin and Assata were already descending the stone steps. Raya and Brother Kane ran past Grim and took the stairs at pace. Grim moved across, blocking the entrance, his back to the stairs, facing a mob of angry orcs. Surely not many fewer than a hundred.

Og held his pike out and the orcs looked warily at the weapon, only too aware that it could take out the first of them to attack. Carefully, Grim felt with his left foot, moving it backwards until it was off the ground. He reached down until he found the first step and was confident enough to put his weight on it. Down he went, while Og and Dog waved their weapons menacingly at the orcs that surrounded them. The creatures spat and threatened but still didn't attack. Down the next step Grim took them, then again, finding the manoeuvre a little more comfortable each time. An orc threw a spear at them, but Dog knocked it aside with his mace and barked ferociously.

Another step down, then another. The orcs remained at the top of the stairs.

'They're not going to follow us,' said Og.

'It would seem not,' said Grim, gingerly turning around on the stairs until at last he could see where he was going. 'Which is both good and bad news.'

'How is it bad?' Og demanded.

'Because it suggests they're too scared of whatever inhabits the next level of the dungeon.'

DEEPWOOD DUNGEON: LEVEL THREE

Before they even got to the bottom of the stairs, Og-Grim-Dog knew what inhabited the next level.

'Trolls,' Dog warned the party.

Troll dung was the foulest odour in all the lands and this part of the dungeon reeked of it. There was never an ogre who had any time for trolls. It was an enmity that stretched back for as long as the two races had co-existed. Goblins and orcs rarely bothered ogres: respecting their strength, they were more inclined to befriend and cooperate with them, though generally gave them a wide berth. Trolls, though. Maybe they were too similar—competing for the same resources. An ogre was more than a match for any single troll. Two trolls, though, were able to turn the tables. And trolls tended to live in groups of three to six, whereas ogres were solitary. It meant that trolls almost always had the upper hand. When they came across the scent of ogre, they would hunt, until their quarry was dead or had escaped from the trolls' territory. It made them the biggest threat to their kind, and Og-Grim-Dog shared every ogre's hatred for them.

Grim had to sense, as much as see, that their friends waited for them where the steps ended.

'I suggest we play this carefully,' Gurin's voice came to them through the darkness.

Good, thought Grim. The dwarf didn't need telling how dangerous trolls could be.

'I'm going to pass you my rope. When everyone has a grip on it, I'm going to move off. If at all possible, we want to find the treasure hoard without alerting the creatures to our presence.'

When they were ready, Gurin inched forwards and the rest followed him. They were even more reliant on the dwarf's eyes now, and Grim wondered once more whether he was partly working from memory. Grim was at the back, behind Raya, and he left a decent space ahead of himself so that he didn't accidentally tread on her. Again, it was his other senses rather than his vision, that told him they were walking down a corridor. The ground underfoot felt like packed dirt and the walls and ceiling had the smell of earth and rot. Ahead, he heard the squeak of a door.

'Stop!' his friends whispered ahead of him and they waited while the dwarf inspected a room.

Waiting in the pitch black is never fun. Your senses can play tricks on you. Grim's mind told him he could hear trolls, but it was just the breathing of his brothers, and the nervous fidgeting of one of his friends up ahead. Although it had felt like a long time, when he felt a pull on the rope, he knew that Gurin's inspection had been brief, and that there must have been little of interest in the room.

They moved on, guiding each other around a corner, and continued along an equally dark corridor. Og-Grim-Dog were the first to hear it—more attuned, perhaps, to the sound of trolls. The dull thud of clumsy feet; the animal grunts; the sound of clubs being dragged along the ground.

'They're coming, from behind us,' Grim whispered hoarsely, hoping it was loud enough to carry to his friends.

A few strangled swear words from the darkness ahead indicated that they did. They moved faster. It was hard to tell in the echoey underground how close the trolls were, or whether they were gaining on them.

'In here,' Gurin hissed.

Grim followed the dwarf's voice and found himself being ushered through a door into a dungeon room.

'I'm going to lead them away,' Gurin told them. 'When they've gone, keep searching for the treasure. Take it straight back to the stairs we came down. Don't try to find me. I'll find you.'

With that, he shut the door on them. If it was dark in the corridor, it was darker here. Grim felt the closeness of his friends, surmising that it was only a small room. The intense aroma of innards hung heavily in the air. He was positioned by the door and he could hear the thud of the trolls getting louder as they drew near. There were many feet.

'I guess five,' Og whispered, clearly thinking along the same lines.

They heard Gurin's full-blooded war cry.

'Come and get fucked by my axe, you shits!'

Then they heard the trolls running past their door after him, the anger in their animal grunts all too clear.

They waited in the darkness for a while, until they were sure that the coast was clear. Grim heard a rustling noise and then a flicker of light appeared as Assata lit her oil lamp. It revealed the room to them. It was indeed small: a storeroom, with foodstuffs packed on shelves and against walls. A wooden barrel was positioned in one corner and Grim could tell that the smell of the room emanated from there. The room suggested more organisational ability than Grim was willing to allow mindless trolls.

'Not tucking in, Og-Grim-Dog?' Raya asked them, one hand covering her nose.

'Not interested in troll leftovers,' said Dog dismissively.

Og opened the door and they exited onto the corridor. Assata led them forwards, oil lamp in one hand, sword in the other. There was no sign or noise of trolls, or Gurin. Assata's lamp soon cast its flickering light on a set of large double doors set into the right wall of the corridor ahead of them. Constructed of long planks of wood and banded with metal, they were a step up in construction from anything else they had seen on this level of the dungeon. Wordlessly, the group looked at one another. There was a very high chance that the treasure of the dungeon would be behind those doors.

They crept quietly to the doors and began to reorganise themselves. Brother Kane took the lamp from Assata and held it up while everyone else in the party readied weapons. Assata pushed at each door, but they were both locked. Raya took out the key she had found in the guardroom on the top level. With a click, the door on the right unlocked. She stepped back again, putting away the key and readying her bow.

Grim stepped into the empty space. With a nod from his friends to say they were ready, he barged the door open and charged into the room. His eyes took in the room of a wealthy troll lord. A large bed lay against the far wall. Spread around it was a considerable treasure horde. Chests held the promise of unknown riches. But even if they were discounted, there was enough coin, precious gems and items of value strewn about the floor to make this a very lucrative dungeon raid.

There was one problem, however. Atop the bed were two trolls. The first, Grim assumed, was the troll lord himself. He was a big unit and was quick to get to his feet, his huge club coming to hand instantly. The second was a female. She moved nearly as fast and grabbed a weapon of her own.

Grim had no more time for thinking. This was going to be difficult. He made for the troll lord, trusting that the others would be able to hold off the second troll until he was done. The troll came for him, too, its huge club held in its long, muscled arm. Grim knew he must stay clear of that weapon at all cost. A clean strike from that would kill in an instant. From the corner of his eye he saw an arrow thud into the chest of the other troll. He doubted that would do much to stop it. But he couldn't worry about that any more as the clash with the troll lord neared.

In a surprise move, Dog threw his mace at the troll. Acting through instinct, the troll lifted his club to bat away the flying mace. That movement was enough for Grim, though, who now knew the troll wouldn't be able to launch a full swing at them for the next few seconds. He launched himself at the troll, hoping that his brothers would act. They did. Og dropped his pike and they both reached out to grab at the troll as they crashed into it. Ogre and troll went tumbling over together, a thrashing mass of heads and limbs. Dog got his hand about the troll's neck. Og tried to do the same, but the troll had found his arm and was strong enough to keep it away.

Grim got one foot against the ground and pushed himself up and on to the troll. His forehead came crashing down and landed on the troll's huge nose with a satisfying crunch of bone. It was enough to loosen its grip on Og's arm and now both of Grim's brothers had their hands about the troll's neck. Grim knew it was over. He heard the snapping of vertebrae as those huge fingers and thumbs squeezed through muscle. The windpipe was crushed, and when they loosened their grip this lord of trolls flopped down, dead.

But Grim knew there was no time to savour a victory and shouted at his brothers to help him up. Getting to his feet, he saw the other troll surrounded by his friends. Raya was fitting an arrow to her bow, the feathered ends of her other missiles protruding from the female troll. Sandon muttered inconsequentially at a spell, while Brother Kane held up the oil lamp, as if helping the others to see the creature was a great benefit. Clearly, therefore, it was Assata who had done the lion's share of the work.

As Grim staggered over to help her, he saw the barbarian duck under a wild swing from the troll. She took the opening, thrusting her sword into its belly, pulling out guts. She stood, admiring her work.

'Move!' Grim shouted at her.

No doubt such a strike had finished every other enemy the barbarian had encountered, but trolls were tough bastards and there was no guarantee it was done. Assata turned to him when she heard the shout, still rooted to the spot. She didn't see the club come around and take her full in the chest. Assata sailed into the air and landed on the floor of the room, her body broken.

'No!' shouted Grim, who went for the troll. Somehow, Og had picked up his pike and he now plunged the blade into the troll. She went to ground, unmoving.

Grim turned to Assata. The others had gathered around her unmoving body. Her eyes were closed and her face an ashen colour.

'I killed her!' Grim lamented. 'I shouldn't have called out like that!'

'Nothing to worry about,' said Sandon. 'I once met a sprite of Terendael Forest, who was immeasurably wise in the ways of elemental magic—'

'Please,' said Brother Kane, gently levering the wizard to one side. 'Let me.'

The cleric placed both hands to the place where the troll's club had fractured the barbarian's chest.

'Mighty Baal, Lord of the Earth and Heavens, Giver of Life and Death, this humble servant calls on you with urgent need.'

There was no made up language now, Grim noticed. Just a direct, heartfelt plea to a higher being.

'Save this Assata; she still has much to offer the world of the living. If you do this, we will both be in your debt.'

A shimmering of silver and golden light appeared then, where Brother Kane's hands met Assata's injury. When the light faded, Assata was wide-eyed and awake, her colour returned. Kane and Raya pulled her into a seating position.

'Praise Baal,' Grim found himself muttering.

Assata met Brother Kane's eyes. 'Thank you,' she said simply.

The cleric smiled his beatific smile, and all was well. Whatever his earlier opinion of the man, Grim had now witnessed him save Assata's life, and he would always be grateful to him for that.

'Well,' said Dog. 'I don't mean to be rude, but there's a lot of treasure in here and we can't be sure that more trolls aren't headed our way. I think we need to get on with it.'

He was right, of course, and they all rushed over to the loot and began filling their knapsacks. Many of the chests turned out to be full, too, and there would be a lot to carry.

'It's a good thing we finished all our food,' Dog muttered happily as he scooped up handfuls of coin. 'It's left more room for treasure.'

Indeed, the ogre's bag was substantially larger than anyone else's and meant that virtually the entire horde could be carried away.

'Anything obviously magical needs to go in here,' said Raya, wafting a bag. She caught Og-Grim-Dog's expressions. 'Don't worry,' she added. 'We can sort it out later.'

When they were done, they were quick to leave the room and shut the doors behind them. Brother Kane, still holding the oil lamp, led them back the way they had come. Sandon was close behind him. Assata was uncertain on her feet, and Og held her under one arm, keeping her upright. At the back of the group, Raya kept an eye out in case any trolls came at them from the rear.

But they heard no more of trolls, and soon they were climbing back up the steps from the troll's level up to where the orcs lived.

The sound of running feet behind them made them all turn. It was Gurin, scampering after them, seemingly none the worse for wear.

'Well?' he demanded with a scowl.

'We got the lot,' said Raya.

Maybe it was the flickering light from Brother Kane's oil lamp, but Grim could have sworn he saw the dwarf crack a smile.

WIGHT'S HOLLOW

They left the Deepwood and made their way to the next dungeon on the list. Wight's Hollow.

'I ain't dealing with no undead,' Dog warned the group as they entered the Moors of Misery.

'Don't worry,' Raya said. 'If there ever was a wight in the caves there, it's long gone now. More goblins and orcs on the menu, I suspect.'

'You may have been spoilt by Deepwood,' Gurin suggested to them. 'Wight's Hollow is a rather ordinary affair.'

The Moors were wet, and the moisture found its way under cloaks and through leather, to irritate, rub and chafe the skin. Grim was not immune, his feet becoming sore from carrying a three-headed ogre around by themselves. He muttered to himself under his breath, but he knew he would get no sympathy. His brothers, Og and Dog, *were* immune. They had never suffered from sore feet. But if he complained, they would simply say he was lucky to have feet. And of course, they were right. So he muttered to himself, while Og slept and Dog told stories.

'The last time we encountered the supernatural was a funny affair. Remember, Grim?'

'Aye,' Grim replied curtly. Maybe it was his sore feet talking, but he didn't recall the experience as being in the slightest bit funny.

'I got myself bitten. I guess that's a whole other story, feisty little ogress she was!'

Grim cleared his throat loudly, hoping it was enough of a signal for Dog to move on.

'Anyway, turned out I got more than I bargained for. She was a werewolf.'

'Really?' Raya asked, putting a hand over her mouth to suppress a giggle.

'Yes. Next full moon, I turned. Spent the rest of the week trying to rip out Grim's throat until he and Og located a witch who cured me. Remember, Grim?'

'I'm hardly going to forget that, am I?' Grim answered irritably.

Raya wasn't even pretending not to laugh anymore, and Assata and Sandon were joining in as well.

'For some reason,' said Grim angrily, 'having a slavering werewolf connected to me for a week, never more than a few inches from my face, constantly trying to sink its teeth into my neck, was not a great source of amusement to me.'

But the angrier he got, the funnier they all found it.

*

It must have been a gradual change, because Grim had not noticed any particular moment when it happened, but he found he was now walking on rocks, not moorland. The ground rose steadily. A cliff face began to materialise ahead of them; it was the dull grey colour of ogre skin, but at the base was a gaping black maw, as unmistakeable an entrance to a dungeon as you might find. Unlike Deepwood Dungeon, this had all the hallmarks of a natural formation, opening onto caves that must have been occupied ever since the first two-legged beings had made their way into Gal'azu.

They stopped by the entrance, reorganising themselves. Walking clothes were swapped for armour, and weapons were taken in hand, or at least placed within easy reach.

'Well?' Assata said, a nervousness in her voice. 'Are we ready?'

They followed the barbarian to the dark cavern. A large opening in the cliff was revealed, stretching back much farther than Grim could see. The roof of the cavern was higher than Og or Dog could reach with their hands, but they could have touched it with their weapons. They entered, looking about them anxiously, wary of traps or an ambush. But the cavern was quiet and the only thing Grim could see was rock.

'If I remember correctly,' said Gurin from the front of the group, 'there is a sizeable drop coming up. We had to climb down using rope to get to the dungeon proper last time.'

They walked a little farther before Gurin called out a warning. 'Careful, now. We need to take a proper look around us. Let me get my torch.'

'No need, friend dwarf,' Sandon declared. 'In the Magicians' Tower in Quar-Del-Prin I studied the fire magic of the Ancient Lords Elemental. There I learned the implorations required to prevail upon the mighty demons of Tzitzuan to grant me the power to make fire and heat from the atmosphere around me. Should they be willing to listen and take heed of my supplications, all that is required is a click of my fingers and a flame shall appear.' The wizard cleared his throat. 'Oh Mighty, Haughty Demons of Tzitzuan—'

'It's alright, Sandon,' Assata said.

The barbarian had lit her oil lamp and she now waved it about them.

Grim could see that the floor of the cavern did indeed suddenly end in what looked like a sizeable drop down into darkness. But he also saw some kind of wooden structure attached to the edge. 'What's that?' he asked. Unable to point, Grim thrust his neck forwards until the others looked in the right direction.

Gurin went over to look, while Assata held her lamp close by.

'Oh,' the dwarf said, sounding disappointed. 'Someone's built some netting onto the side of the rock. Looks like it's been nailed in securely. If it holds, it should be easy enough to climb down. I was rather hoping that we would be using rope. More of a challenge than this.'

'Or I could have used my teleportation spell,' said Sandon wistfully. 'Been a while since I deployed that particular tool in my armoury. It's a shame really, because I spent a good two years perfecting its use. This was back when I lived amongst the—'

'I'll go first,' said Assata, handing her lamp to Gurin and pulling hard at the netting to make sure it would take her weight. She swung one leg over the edge of the drop, getting her first foot secure. Then she was off, grabbing it with her hands, while her second foot explored downwards. She moved quickly, strong and agile as a cat. Gurin held the torch over the edge so they could see her. But before long she had disappeared down into the darkness and Raya had scrambled onto the netting. Nimble as a squirrel, if anything she disappeared even faster.

Sandon and Brother Kane went next, neither of them as comfortable looking with the prospect of clinging to a rock face above what was probably a huge drop down.

'Just as well I can't see to the bottom,' the wizard gasped, his limbs trembling.

Brother Kane maintained his beatific smile, though in the torchlight he did look a lot paler than usual.

'I would suggest,' Grim said to Gurin, 'that you go next. There is no knowing whether that netting can hold our weight.'

The dwarf looked them over and nodded in silent agreement. He put out the lamp and returned it to his pack, then began scrambling down.

Three ogre heads peered over the ledge at the netting.

'Now then,' said Og. 'This could be something of a challenge. We're not the most co-ordinated of creatures.'

'We can do it,' Grim assured him. 'Slow and steady; one limb at a time. We each tell the others when we have lifted a hand or a foot off, and when it is back down. Then the next one takes his turn.'

The three brothers had their share of disagreements and arguments. But self-preservation is a strong instinct and hanging off a sheer rock face on a flimsy-feeling piece of hemp netting helped to concentrate their minds. They worked together and they held their tempers. Perhaps just as remarkably, the netting held their weight and they reached the bottom in one piece.

Their friends had waited for them at the foot of the rock. Grim could sense that they were in a vast chamber, even if he couldn't see more than a few feet ahead. They left, making their way through the darkness of the underworld. The sound of boots on the floor echoed. In many places Grim found he was walking on a thick layer of guano, and the sharp smell of bat urine was pervasive.

Gurin led them into a tunnel. There was something comforting to Grim about being closed in by walls and a roof. Assata pointed to locations farther along the tunnel—doors. The denizens of the dungeon might be close.

They continued on, Grim doing his best to move quietly. In what was now becoming a familiar routine, Gurin and Assata stood on each side of a wooden door and silently invited Grim to burst it open. He obliged, kicking it open and entering the room at speed. It was a reasonably sized room, with an open exit on the right wall into a second room. In the gloom, Grim could make out odd bits of furniture lining the walls. Against one wall, something stirred.

'Hold it!' Assata demanded, levelling her sword at the creature.

It was an orc. He was seated on top of a cushion, a filthy-looking blanket wrapped about him, his back against the wall. He had a startled expression on his face and raised his arms in alarm.

'Oh, you got me,' he said in a throaty voice. 'I must have dozed off and didn't hear you coming.'

'Anyone else around here?' Assata demanded.

'Oh, I doubt it. They'll all have run off when they knew you were coming. Look at you, swords and bows and a great big ogre, too. No, they'll be long gone.'

'Nothing in there,' Gurin confirmed, exiting the adjoining room. 'We need to finish that one.'

'Oh, no need for that!' said the orc. 'I've been poorly, that's why I was dozing off here. I'm no threat to you. I'll just stay here until you're done. You won't hear a peep from me. I'm Vax, by the way.'

'We can't trust orcs,' said Gurin, brandishing his axe.

Assata and the others looked unsure about what to do with the orc. Grim did think it would be a poor show to just kill the old thing in cold blood. But then, that was what trespassers tended to do in these situations. Kill all the residents and take the loot.

'What about that piece of rope you never used?' Og asked Gurin.

'What about it?' replied the dwarf suspiciously.

'Tie him up with it.'

'He'll call out.'

'Gag him.'

'We came here to kill orcs, didn't we?' Gurin demanded.

'Not really,' said Assata, as if she had at last made a decision. 'We came here to grab back the treasure they've been stealing.'

'And killing people while they did it,' Gurin countered. 'Killing innocent humans. Women and children.'

'Oh, no,' said Vax. 'That wasn't us. You must have us mistaken with some other orcs.'

'The rope,' Assata said, holding out a hand.

With a reluctant sigh, the dwarf handed the barbarian his rope. She tied it tightly around the orc.

'If we hear you cry out or make any kind of noise, I'll send the dwarf to get his rope back. Do you understand what I'm saying?'

'Oh yes,' Vax said. 'You've been very kind. Though I feel I should warn you.'

'Oh yeah?'

'You won't find much in the way of treasure down here.'

'We'll see,' Gurin said with a sneer.

They left the orc behind and gave the other tunnel rooms a search. But it was just as Vax had said: no-one else was about and none of the rooms held anything of value. Indeed, they were exceedingly grubby looking, even for orcs, and it seemed obvious to Grim that these creatures had fallen on hard times.

When they were done, they found themselves at the end of the tunnel, where it sloped and turned downwards, towards the next level.

'Well, only a single orc on the whole top level,' said Dog.

'Let's see what we find down here, before we dismiss the whole dungeon,' said Gurin.

But Grim thought that the dwarf didn't sound so confident anymore.

DISCOUNT DUNGEON SUPPLIES

The tunnel carried them down at a gentle gradient, twisting around so that they emerged directly under the passage they had just walked through. The sight before them here, however, was very different. Instead of a narrow tunnel, there was a large open space. At the far end Grim could see the passage that led down to the next floor. But like everyone else, his attention was drawn to the centre of the open space. Brightly illuminated, a shop had been built there. To be precise, it was a branch of Discount Dungeon Supplies.

'Rather odd,' said Sandon.

'This!' Gurin said. Grim looked at the dwarf. His face had gone red and he seemed to be having trouble getting his words out. 'This symbolises all that has gone wrong with modern dungeoneering!' he said finally. 'A shop! In the middle of a dungeon! What kind of soft, supine, shameless, waste of space goes shopping in the middle of a dungeon crawl? What kind of sick, consumer-obsessed society have we become?'

He stared about him, as if someone would be able to answer the question. It seemed that no-one could, since an awkward silence followed.

'Are we going to go in?' asked Raya eventually.

'Well—' said Sandon. 'It's right here, so...'

'Maybe we can find out some information?' Assata suggested. 'Obviously, we're not going to *buy* anything,' she added, looking at the dwarf a little sheepishly.

'It's alright,' Gurin said to Og-Grim-Dog. 'You go in with them.' The dwarf sat on the floor and crossed his arms.

'I'll stay with Gurin,' said Brother Kane. 'We'll keep a watch.'

The rest of them entered the shop. It was well lit inside, just like the outside. Two guards were stationed there. They were heavily armoured, each carrying a spear and shield. A third man stood at the counter. Otherwise, it was empty. The shop seemed to stock everything a dungeon adventurer might need: cloaks hung on hangers; there were shoes in different styles and sizes; leather and metal armour for all parts of the body; round shields, kite shields and bucklers. There were shelves full of essentials and miscellaneous items: dried food; water bottles; backpacks; lengths of rope; flint, steel and tinderboxes; medical supplies.

But pride of place, and the part of the shop they all gravitated to, were the weapon racks. There was every type of weapon Grim had ever heard of, and some he hadn't, each with a different price tag. Cheap items such as staves, clubs and fire-hardened spears. Swords of different lengths and shapes, each going for eye-watering prices. Bows and a selection of arrows; slings and stones. Exotic items, such as darts, morningstars, battle hammers. They stood about for a little while, pointing things out to each other. 'Here, Dog, look at this.' 'Assata, you should get one of these.' And so on.

For Grim, it was a bittersweet display. For while the weapons were enticing, he knew he would never get to hold one, let alone use any of them in anger.

Eventually, the man behind the counter sidled over. 'Anything I can help you with?'

'We're just looking,' said Raya.

'Are you the manager?' Assata asked the man.

'Indeed I am. Simon Granger, at your service.'

The manager of the shop offered his hand and Assata shook it.

'Why *did* they open a shop in the middle of a dungeon?'

'It was my idea, actually,' Simon replied. 'It's a franchise.'

Everyone looked at him blankly.

'So, I thought, why not have a store, right where adventurers such as yourselves need it? Say you lose or break a weapon? Or face some danger and wish you had a set of iron spikes, or a length of rope? Someone in your party gets injured, and needs medicine? Or, rather than having to carry all your victuals, you can pick it up conveniently here? That's my idea. The franchise angle means that I am the owner of the store. Discount Dungeon Supplies helped me to set it up, they supply the merchandise, and in return they get a cut of the profits I make. I like to think it's a scheme where everyone wins.'

'Are you making much money?' Grim asked him.

Simon's face turned a little glum. 'Well, starting a new business is never easy. But if I start to sell some of the big-ticket items, things might pick up. Footfall is also an issue. I'm trying to make it easier for adventurers to get here.'

'That netting up the rock. That was you?' Grim asked him.

'Yes. The more adventurers who make it this far, the more customers I get.'

'The lights?'

Simon pointed up at the ceiling of the shop where numerous small lights shone down at regular intervals.

'Glow-worms. Supplied by head office. They really are quite something, aren't they?'

'But what about the dungeon monsters?' Sandon asked, his features creased in puzzlement. 'Why haven't they destroyed this place and taken everything inside?'

'Well, relations with them can be tense. Ernst and Gernot over there,' he said, gesturing at the armed guards, 'keep out the riffraff. I lock the place up at night.' He paused, studying them. Grim fancied he was debating with himself whether to say more. 'I have had to make a deal or two with some of the residents of the dungeon. Give them a cut. But again, that means everyone wins.'

'And I suppose you have to pay the guards their wages?' Assata asked him.

'Yes. They mind the store and get me to and from the dungeon.'

Grim was thinking—about their secret quest, to find out why the trespassers kept coming to their dungeon and killing orcs.

'Surely, if you want to attract adventurers here, you need it filled with monsters and treasure. But the floor we just passed through was virtually deserted. And the more dungeon dwellers there are here, the more guards you would have to employ, and the more of them you would need to pay off. Something about this store doesn't quite make sense.'

'I think I understand it,' said Assata. 'He doesn't want *real* adventurers here. Like us. He's making a tourist dungeon. A theme park. Soon he'll have a stable up by the entrance, with a proper road leading to it. It will be ticket entry, and the netting on the rock will be replaced by baskets with seats that get winched down to the top floor of the dungeon. The orc rooms we searched through will be converted into toilets and baby changing facilities. There'll be snack huts everywhere. Long queues to meet an orc or a goblin while an artist draws your picture with it. Gurin was right. This is the death of real dungeon crawling.'

They all looked at Simon. At least he didn't try to protest. They turned to go.

'Is there nothing you want to purchase?' he asked pleadingly. 'I could do you a group discount.'

Assata and Sandon turned their backs on him and left the shop.

Raya sighed. 'You need some food, Og-Grim-Dog?'

'Ooh, yes please,' said Dog.

They grabbed some of the provisions and took them to the counter.

'I'll take that set of arrows, too,' she said to Simon, and handed over the money.

'Thank you for your business,' he said.

Og-Grim-Dog and Raya left the store to join the others. They were talking together quietly, in solemn voices. They turned at the approach of the ogre and elf.

'We were thinking it might be best just to leave,' said Assata.

No-one argued.

THE CRUSHED GRAPES IN URLAY

After the elation of Deepwood Dungeon, Wight's Hollow had been a let-down. But the company held strong. There was no talk of giving up, and instead they began to make for the third dungeon on their list.

'The Sargassian Empire was one of the very first realms of men,' said Sandon, as they left the dark maw of the cavern behind them and travelled east. 'Old and mysterious, it fell, like all empires do, a long time ago. The Crimson Palace is a magnificent remnant of the Empire, said to have been the home of the ruling dynasty for hundreds of years. Three hundred steps take you to the top of a great mound and the entrance to the palace. Great artefacts of power have been found by those who dared to descend to the lowest levels. It is said that there are still some yet to be found.'

'Is it far?' Grim asked.

'No,' said Sandon, looking a little disappointed with the question. But the truth was, Grim's legs were killing him. He hadn't done this much walking for years. 'We will be there in two days,' the wizard answered.

Grim made a face.

'I know a place where we can stop,' said the wizard. 'A nice inn, by a river. Maybe we deserve a rest.'

Gurin's face darkened. 'I don't think we should be making detours.'

'Come on, Gurin,' said Assata. 'I think we need a decent bed and a warm meal. Get our spirits up.'

The dwarf harrumphed at that but didn't argue. For the first time, Sandon led the group.

*

'The village of Urlay,' said Sandon, waving down at the valley beneath them.

'What happened to it?' asked Raya.

'What do you mean?' said the wizard, staring at the settlement.

Grim looked down as well, but it was too far away to see much more than a smudge of buildings huddled along the river. Too far to see for most creatures.

'Elven eyes,' Dog muttered darkly.

'Half the houses look damaged, if not totally shattered,' Raya added. 'Something unpleasant happened here.'

They descended the valley, a shared sense of foreboding smothering any conversation. As they neared the buildings, Grim could see that several of the wooden structures had been gutted by fire. Normally, human settlements would be a hive of activity, much of it related to farming. Humans seemed to insist on carrying out various jobs related to making plants and animals grow. Grim was under the impression that plants and animals generally tended to grow by themselves, without the need for intervention, but he didn't pretend to understand human ways. Anyway. Not a single villager could be seen.

'That's the inn,' Sandon said, pointing at the most substantial building in the village. It still stood, taking pride of place in the village. Its spacious front yard led on to the river jetty, but there were no boats moored up.

'Let's take a look,' Assata suggested.

The Crushed Grapes was an attractive, stone-built affair, large enough to cater to big groups, presumably river traders. The outside of the building was unharmed—even the wooden sign, depicting a bunch of purple grapes, still swung gently in the breeze. For whatever reason, the raiders who had come here appeared to have left the inn intact. They entered the lounge area. The furniture was laid out ready for guests, though the room was empty.

A clanging noise came from the direction of the kitchen. Looking at one another, the group headed that way. An archway led into the kitchen, where they found a lone human woman preparing food. She had her back to them and didn't hear them come in at first. When she turned around, she gave a shriek of fear and grabbed a kitchen knife, waving it at them.

'Whoah, steady now,' said Assata. 'We're not here to harm you.'

'What are they doing here?' the woman said hysterically. Not unsurprisingly, her knife jabbed in Og-Grim-Dog's direction.

'Why don't you all wait back there, while I speak to her?' Assata suggested.

It sounded sensible, and so the five of them retreated to the lounge. Raya investigated the bar. 'They have wine,' she said. Grim wondered if she was making an effort to keep her voice casual. 'I'm sure they won't mind us helping ourselves and leaving a payment,' she decided.

The elf fixed everyone a drink and they all took a seat, waiting for Assata to calm the human down. After a while, the barbarian brought the woman into the lounge with her. They were talking quietly together, though Assata managed to cast over a frown at her fellow adventurers, presumably because they were all supping The Crushed Grapes' wine. Which wasn't half bad.

'I saw them from behind the bar, here,' the woman was saying. She led Assata round to the serving side of the bar. 'They were down by the river. No-one else had seen them. But this side of the bar is raised, see? And I caught a glimpse of their heads.'

'Whose heads?' Sandon asked, sounding intrigued.

The woman looked across at Sandon, nervous looking.

'This is Betty, the landlady,' said Assata.

'I know. Hullo Betty. I'm Sandon. I've been a guest here before. You might remember me?'

Betty shrugged. 'Maybes.'

'Whose heads did you see?' Sandon asked, keeping his voice light.

'The orcs.'

'Orcs did this?' Grim asked.

'Yes,' said the woman.

'And what did everyone in the inn do?'

'We got the cellar door open and hid inside. Got all the children and old ones in first, then we decided we'd all hide down there.'

'And the orcs didn't visit the inn?' Grim asked. 'They just went for the houses?'

'Orcs are cowards,' Gurin said dismissively. 'They'll have bypassed the inn, thinking they might meet too much resistance here.'

'Where's everyone now?' Sandon asked the woman.

'My husband and most of the menfolk set off downriver for Dorwich City. There's a reeve there who might raise a force and come here to help. That was over a week ago now. Left me here to look after the kids and the poorly. They're still down in the cellar, too scared to come up. I have some help, but it's been hard. And I'm fearing in case them orcs come back!'

Assata gave the landlady a reassuring pat on the shoulder. The conversation drifted on to other things, but the exchange stuck with Grim. He wandered out of The Crushed Grapes for some fresh air.

'I know that face, Grim,' said Og, looking at him. 'It's your thinking face.'

'Queen Krim asked us to find out why the orcs of Darkspike Dungeon were being targeted,' Grim began. 'And this kind of thing might explain it.'

'Of course,' agreed Dog, knocking back the last of his wine. 'What else might a king's reeve, with a posse of thirty-odd men do, but go and take it out on the orcs from the nearest dungeon?'

'Yes. But something doesn't feel right. Queen Krim told us her orcs were too weakened to go out raiding. And think of what we found at the Deepwood and Wight's Hollow. Not enough orcs there, either, to risk something like this.'

'True, Grim,' Og said. 'I knew you were thinking.'

'And not only that,' said Grim. 'The orcs who raided this village ignored the inn, where they were sure to find all the drink and food and travellers with their possessions? Instead, they target the houses of the ordinary village folk—you wouldn't expect to find much of value there, would you? Doesn't seem like normal orc behaviour to me.'

'Now you mention it, Grim,' Dog said, 'it is all starting to sound kind of suspicious. What are you thinking then? Some kind of conspiracy going on, eh? The government, probably. Possibly aliens, too.'

'Well,' said Grim, ignoring the last comment, 'something doesn't feel right, that's all. I haven't managed to work out what it is yet, though.'

Dog sighed. 'For a second there, Grim, I thought you were gonna solve the case, and it would be all dramatic and exciting. But all you've got is 'something don't feel right'. Come on, let's get back inside, can we? There's still some of that wine left and if we don't keep an eye on it, that elf will guzzle the lot.'

But Grim wasn't yet ready to return to the inn. He walked over to the riverbank. This was where the landlady had seen the orc raiders and there might still be clues here.

Just as the thought crossed his mind, a metallic glint caught his eye. There was something buried in the mud of the riverbank.

'Fetch that out for me, will you Og?' he asked once he had walked over to take a closer look.

'Ouch!' said Og as he grabbed at it. 'It's sharp!'

Og now dug around the buried item until he was able to pull it up without cutting himself.

'A knife?' Dog asked.

'I would say more like a sword, if we are talking orc-size,' said Og, wafting the weapon about. It had the distinctive broad-headed blade favoured by orcs. But the hilt was intricately made, with a curved cross-guard and a striking red grip.

'An interesting item,' Grim commented.

Dog rolled his eyes. 'Come on, Grim. Investigating conspiracies is fun as far as it goes. But I have already mentioned that my wine cup is empty.'

Reluctantly, Grim returned to the inn. Dog was right, he hadn't solved a mystery. Hadn't even got close. But still. He knew he was on to something.

INTERMISSION

The Landlord knew how to tell a story and he knew how to judge an audience. This was an audience that needed a toilet break halfway through, and so he paused the story for a little while. And why not take a few orders while he did so? The drinkers at the Flayed Testicles agreed with one another that listening to this story was thirsty work.

In this way the ordinary noise of an evening inn returned, when before all had been silent, except for the words of the storyteller and the scratch of the Recorder's quill on parchment. A myriad of small conversations began, chairs were scraped across the floor, mugs were clinked as they were returned to the bar.

The Landlord, whose customers now knew to be the infamous ogre Og-Grim-Dog, poured drinks and took money.

The Recorder also remained busy. He sprinkled sand onto his parchment to dry out the ink, then sprinkled pounce onto a fresh piece to prepare it for the resumption. Some of the regulars anxiously peered over his shoulder at the writing, wondering how he did. For no-one had forgotten the ogre's threat to kill everyone inside the Testicles should the Recorder fail in his task. Those who took a peep were neither relieved nor worried by what they saw, since it hadn't been made at all clear what would constitute failure and what success. The regulars knew that words had been spoken and words had been written down. Beyond that, they were none the wiser.

Eventually, the inn settled. Uninstigated, a hush descended on the Flayed Testicles, that let the Landlord know it was time to resume.

Three pairs of ogre eyes scanned the room, as if looking for something.

'Now, where were we?' asked the third head.

The Recorder scanned his notes. 'You had just arrived at the village of Urlay and discovered that it had been attacked by an orc raiding party. I presume this has some significance to the story.'

The ogre frowned at him. 'Of course it does. Otherwise, we wouldn't have mentioned it, would we?'

'Oh, that's good. I was just a little concerned that the story might be drifting off into irrelevance. After all, let's see.' The Recorder flicked through his notes. 'Yes, here. You said that your party had signed up to visit six dungeons, and so far you have only told us about two. And it already feels like it's starting to drag a little bit? I don't know,' he said, looking about the inn for support. 'Maybe that's just me?'

The ogre scowled at the man. 'Well, if you had given us a chance to get a word in,' said the second head, 'you would have known that we never intended to go into detail on the other four dungeons. Suffice it to say, that our experiences there met the same pattern as we had found in the first two. Starting with the Crimson Palace, none of the others provided such a stiff test as the Deepwood. None were quite so pitiful as Wight's Hollow, though they resembled the latter more than the former. In each one, the opposition we found was limited, and the numbers of orcs few. The loot we found was, on the whole, disappointing.

We rooted out gold coins, some precious gems, the odd stash of weapons and other items that could be sold on. But our fantasies of finding magical swords, lost crowns, ancient wisdom, imprisoned ogre princesses, or whatever other dreams our party had, did not come to pass. So it was that we returned to where we started, the town of Mer Khazer. Alive and well. Better off than when we had left. But a little disappointed, nonetheless.'

THE MYSTERY DEEPENS

They returned to Mer Khazer. The population of the town welcomed them back as heroes. There was music and singing and the stallholders fought to press the finest food into their hands. Og-Grim-Dog loved it. Until Sandon reminded them that they had to pay another visit to the Bureau of Dungeoneering.

All kinds of paperwork now had to be filled in. Since Og-Grim-Dog was carrying most of the loot they had won, the ogre was given the task of dealing with objects, which sounded less complicated than some of the other jobs his friends had. Raya went with him and led him to the appropriate desks.

At Financials, the clerk recorded how much money they had made on their adventure; they also had to decide which items they wanted to keep, and which they would sell on to the Bureau. The clerk at the desk had a long list of objects such as weapons and armour, precious jewels, historic coins and artefacts. In the next column was the prices the Bureau would pay for each. No doubt these would then be sold on to buyers at a profit. Og-Grim-Dog had little sense of money or the cost of things and so let Raya make the decisions. At the end of it, the clerk handed them over several bags of coins—the profits of their dungeon crawl.

'I also have a note,' he said, 'to remind you that Mr Agassi is owed five per cent of your winnings.'

'We remember,' said Grim. 'We'll take the money to him.' He didn't begrudge Mr Agassi the money. They had only gone on their adventure because of his help, and they had never really been in it for the money anyway.

'Why does the Bureau need to know so much about the money we took?' Grim asked the elf as they crossed the office to the next desk.

'Many reasons,' Raya said. 'One of them is that it helps them get a picture of the health of each dungeon. If parties report back that they found little or nothing in a dungeon, they might decide to close it down to adventurers for a while. Let it fill up with monsters and treasure again.'

'But most of them *were* pretty weak sauce,' said Dog. 'Shouldn't we tell somebody?'

'Gurin is over at Applications for Dungeons Crawls,' she said, pointing over to where the dwarf stood in conversation at the desk. 'They record that kind of anecdotal information. Then cross reference it with Financials and any other evidence they have. They're pretty thorough. Right, here we are. Magical Items. We should have a separate bag for this, Og-Grim-Dog. Yes, that one.'

At the Magical Items desk, they needed to hand in anything that might contain a magical charge of some kind.

'It's for safety reasons as much as anything else,' said the witch at the desk, when she learned that Og-Grim-Dog was a new member of the Bureau. 'In the old days we let the adventurers walk off with any old item. Well, we had devils escaping from magical captivity; spectres encased in jewellery or weapons would seize the bodies of their owners. Committed all sorts of vicious atrocities, they did. So now we check everything first. Even if you think there's no magic in it at all, it's always better to be safe than sorry.'

Og-Grim-Dog placed the bag into the box provided. It had strange, colourful markings all over it.

'Covered in anti-magic wards,' the witch explained when she saw the ogre studying the box. 'Come and pick your items up tomorrow,' she said cheerfully.

Once all the administration was done, the team reassembled.

'Tired faces,' Sandon commented as he looked at everyone. 'It hits you when you finally stop.'

'Yes,' Assata agreed. 'I think I'm ready for a sleep in a bed at The Bollocks.'

'But we're going to have a drink in the bar, first?' Raya asked. 'We have to celebrate.'

With different levels of enthusiasm, everyone agreed to the elf's request. But the Bureau had one last surprise for them. As they were leaving, a voice called over from Registration.

'I thought you ought to know.' It was the same woman who had refused to register Og-Grim-Dog in the first place. She had a triumphant looking expression on her face. 'The Bureau has amended the membership rules. Here,' she said, pointing to a passage in a fresh-looking copy of the constitution.

With a sense of foreboding, Grim walked across to the desk, his friends coming with him. The amended passage was easy enough to read. Section four, sub-section two now said: 'Goblins, orcs, trolls, ogres and other such monsters shall, under no condition, be admitted as members of the Bureau of Dungeoneering.'

The voices of his new friends rose in protest around him, but it was as clear as clear could be. Their adventuring days were over. Grim felt more sad than angry.

‘Please don’t,’ he said to Dog, as his brother unclipped his mace from his belt. ‘Killing the official isn’t going to change anything.’

‘It will make me feel better,’ Dog responded, but he returned his weapon to his belt nonetheless.

There was talk of appeals and legal challenges. Assata said she would organise a protest event. But Grim wasn’t in the mood for all that.

‘Come on,’ he said to them. ‘Let’s get to the bar. I’d rather celebrate our successes than talk of this anymore.’

‘If that’s what you want,’ said Raya. ‘I’ll get the first round in.’

☆

Grim couldn’t lie about in bed any longer. His brothers were still inebriated from the night before. But he had to do something.

They left their room at The Bollocks. Og remained asleep. Dog woke up, hungover, and muttered a string of abuse at him. But at least he was roused enough to open doors and such, allowing Grim to leave the inn.

There weren’t many places in Mer Khazer to go. After a while, Grim decided to go the house of Mr Agassi, the lawyer who had won their original case against the Bureau of Dungeoneering. He was entitled to a share of their treasure, and Grim thought they might as well take it to him now.

It was early morning and the ghoul was home, still in his dressing gown. Fortunately for the ogre, Mr Agassi was fixing his breakfast.

‘There’s plenty to go around,’ he said, returning to his kitchen, as Grim settled down onto the floor of the front room. The ghoul soon returned with steaming hot mugs of a meaty broth and a mouth-watering selection of hot meat.

'Fresh off the slab,' the ghoul announced as he placed the meat on the floor next to them.

The tempting smells woke Og up and Grim's two brothers got stuck into breakfast, shoving handfuls of meat and fat and gristle into Grim's mouth for him when their own were too full. When they were finally gorged, it was time to speak.

'Dog, could you give Mr Agassi his fees?'

The ghoul took the bag of money, giving it a little shake.

'You did well!'

'Less than I thought we might get.'

'Income from dungeon crawling has been in decline for some time now. It looks like you did better than most crews.'

'The Bureau has banned ogres from membership.'

'I'm not surprised,' said the ghoul. 'For one, there are too many adventurers these days, and not enough monster-filled dungeons. You might say the industry has become a victim of its own success. And that's not really an environment where people will be welcoming to newcomers. Secondly, of course, you're fighting against millennia of discrimination and hatred from humans. Not an easy thing to overcome. You might want to think yourselves lucky you were ever admitted in the first place. Where you go from here, it's hard for me to advise. I've made a place for myself in human society by making my services valuable enough for clients to ignore what I am. When it comes to disputes of law, all people really want to do is win. They hire the best. Maybe you could do something similar.'

'Who says we even want to make it in human society?' Og demanded. 'Especially if they treat us like this. We were perfectly happy back in our cavern, weren't we?'

'For once, I agree with Og,' said Dog. 'Why does everyone want to act like humans anyway? It's time to get back home, I say.'

'If you both remember,' Grim said, 'we came here to find out why the humans keep attacking the dungeons, even when there's little left to take. In my opinion, we have and we haven't. We know that adventuring is fun and popular, even when there's not so many monsters and treasure as there used to be. But the people are still scared of monsters, especially orcs. The Bureau keeps the dungeons open even when they're beaten into the ground. And villages like Urlay are still getting raided by orcs, even though we haven't found a single orc band strong enough to do it. There's still something yet to solve.'

'Who gives a crap?' Dog demanded. 'We're an ogre. We're not meant to solve mysteries. We're not meant to hang out with wizards and elves and dwarves. We're meant to eat them. This has to stop, Grim.'

'So what? We shrug our shoulders and go back to our cavern?' Grim demanded. 'Wait until all the orcs and goblins are killed? All the trolls are dead? And then a party of heroes comes to our home and kills us? How stupid is that?'

'Let them try and kill us,' Dog said. 'I'll crush their heads in.'

Grim sighed. Dog didn't want to see it. There was no point in arguing.

'You'll have to work it out for yourselves,' said Mr Agassi, with some sympathy.

'Let's at least go back to the Bureau and pick up that bag from Magical Items,' said Grim.

'Alright, Grim,' said Og. 'It's your legs that are doing the walking. Thanks for breakfast, Mr Agassi.'

Mr Agassi waved them off as they left his little terraced street.

Grim returned to the Bureau building, even though it had never been his favourite place. There was someone else on duty at the Magical Items desk, but they agreed to hand back the items once they verified Og-Grim-Dog's identity.

First, the bag was returned, then the clerk reappeared with a tray full of the items they had deposited yesterday. There was a note with it. 'Nothing dangerous,' the clerk said, reading from it. 'There is a Ring of Curse-Breaking. We've put it in an envelope for you. You'll probably want to pass that on to your wizard. Otherwise, everything else is magic-free.'

'Of course,' said Grim. Og and Dog began bundling the items back into the bag.

'Hey, Og,' said Dog. 'What is that sword Grim found in the village doing here? You didn't think that was magical, did you?'

Dog took the weapon in his hand. It had the distinctive broad-headed blade loved by orcs, with the delicately crafted red hilt.

'Eh? I didn't put it in there.' Og patted at his belt, then withdrew the sword. 'See? That's a different one.'

'Wait a minute,' said Grim. A strange thought was struggling to the surface. 'They're identical. Are you sure this sword was in the bag?' he asked the clerk.

'Positive. You're the only group who made a deposit yesterday.'

'So whose is it?' Grim asked.

'Well,' said Og, 'presumably someone found it in one of the dungeons.'

'I think I would have noticed if someone found the exact same weapon in one of the dungeons,' said Grim. 'And I think they would have done too, since we walked into The Crushed Grapes brandishing it for all to see. There's something very odd about this.'

Grim's brothers eyed the two identical weapons.

'I feel like you're right,' Og admitted eventually. 'But what does it mean?'

'What if,' said Grim, his words running at the same pace as his thoughts, 'orcs never attacked that village in Urlay? What if someone else did? And what if the person or persons behind that attack was someone from our party?'

'You mean a treacherous scumbag pretending to be a friend?' asked Dog, anger plain in his voice. 'A liar and a crook, deceiving us, making everyone believe it was orcs doing the killings, when it was them? I say we find out who that someone is.'

'My thoughts exactly,' said Grim. 'But we have to play this clever, because that's how this individual has played it. No giving away our suspicions, or that we've found a second sword. If we act careful, we might uncover the criminal.'

'Maybe they think because we're an ogre, we'll be too stupid to work it out,' said Dog. 'But there's three heads working on this now.'

THE BARBARIAN

You could say it was chance that Assata was the first member of the party that Og-Grim-Dog investigated—certainly, no plan had been formulated. Grim was walking back to The Bruised Bollocks when they saw the barbarian leaving.

'Follow her, Grim,' Og said, sounding excited.

Assata crossed the road and carried on towards a part of town that the ogre had never been to.

'I wonder where she's going,' said Dog, his tone implying that the barbarian was up to no good. Grim was a little concerned that his brothers were now too wrapped up with finding evidence of wrongdoing.

'Careful, Grim,' Dog added. 'Don't get too close.'

Grim slowed down, letting Assata get further ahead of them, but keeping her within sight.

'Now,' said Og. 'What do we have on the barbarian?'

'She doesn't drink,' said Dog. 'That's suspicious in itself. It gives her more time to further her nefarious plans while the rest of us are sleeping off our fug.'

Alright. Now Grim was sure they were taking it too far.

'Good,' said Og. 'What else?'

'Assata was the one who recruited us in the first place, if you recall?' said Dog.

'What does that prove?' demanded Grim. 'Apart from the fact that she didn't treat us with prejudice, like most people do.'

'Fair enough, Grim,' Dog acknowledged. 'It doesn't prove anything. *Necessarily.*'

Grim ignored that, concentrating on his quarry. Assata was leading them away from the town centre with its shops and inns. They were now in a residential area, the human houses squashed together, built from flimsy material.

Then, she disappeared into one of the houses.

'Did you see that, Grim?'

'Yes,' he said, picking up the pace, while keeping the house fixed in his sights. He approached the building, unsure what to do next. Three-headed ogres had their limitations when it came to looking inconspicuous.

'There,' said Og, pointing to an alley on the left. 'I bet that goes behind the house.'

Grim didn't hesitate in taking the alley, sensing eyes observing them. As Og had suggested, the alley branched out in different directions, and one of them took them behind the house that Assata had entered.

'Is that it?' Dog asked, pointing at the dilapidated wooden exterior.

'I think so,' said Grim. It was hard to tell for sure, since the houses all looked the same. 'What now?'

'Wait?' Og offered.

Grim sighed. Their total lack of a plan felt very apparent.

'Wait for what?' asked a voice.

At the same time, the tip of a sword appeared from behind them and nestled between Grim and Dog's necks.

'Oh!' said Og, slightly braver since he didn't have cold steel quite so close. 'Hello, Assata! Erm…fancy seeing you here?'

'You know,' said the barbarian, 'it crossed my mind that you didn't want me to know that you were following me. But since you were talking to one another the whole time, out loud, I discarded the idea.'

'Of course,' Grim squeaked out, nervous of the blade, aware that his reply didn't really make any sense.

'I think you'd better come with me,' said the barbarian, and Og-Grim-Dog didn't argue.

Assata strode over to the house and pulled out a couple of planks of wood. The space she had made was big enough for her to fit through. She looked at the ogre, sizing him up, and took out another couple of planks, before gesturing him inside with her sword.

The inside of the house was dark. A fire in the pit offered more smoke than light. Two figures stood in the shadows, casting the ogre climbing into their house suspicious glances.

'Well,' said Assata, entering behind them, and gesturing to a mat on the floor with her still-drawn sword, 'I presume you wanted to know why I came here.'

'We did,' said Dog, as Grim took a seat on the mat. 'Also, we were wondering what's in the pot,' he added, gesturing at the fire pit.

Assata rolled her eyes, but she strode to the pot anyway, ladling some of the soup into a bowl and handing it to Dog, who took a sniff as the steam rose about him. 'Well-seasoned,' he commented. 'Meat in there?'

'Vegetables.'

'That's fine.'

Assata nodded at the two men who came over to the mat, and all three sat. They all had the same look to them: more than just the features that suggested they were from the same tribe—they had a hardness that said that life had toughened them.

Assata finally laid her sword down on the floor. She pulled up her sleeve and showed them a swirling, ink black symbol on her forearm. 'Do you know what this means?' she asked.

'You like tattoos?' Dog asked.

'No, Dog,' she said. The two men showed the ogre the same tattoo. 'It means we're escaped slaves. The Kuthenian Empire likes barbarians for its slaves, for some reason. Maybe because we look different, and they like to know instantly who is slave and who is free in the Empire. I came here to give the money I made from our dungeon crawl to my friends here. They will take it home for the Resistance. You see, we won't rest until the Kuthenians are brought to their knees and we bathe in their blood.'

'I see,' said Grim. 'I wondered why you asked us to join your adventuring party.'

Assata smiled at him. 'I know that ogres aren't the real monsters. Do ogres keep slaves?'

'Never!' said Og, shocked.

'Although it's an idea,' said Dog.

'Quiet, Dog,' said Grim. 'Drink your soup. I'm sorry it looks like we didn't trust you,' he said to Assata, genuinely ashamed.

Assata made a face, looking at her two associates. 'I suppose we can forgive you. I doubt you meant harm by it. But seriously, what are you up to?'

The brothers looked at one another a little awkwardly.

'It's a difficult matter,' said Grim, unwilling to tell her, but feeling like he really should have.

Assata raised an eyebrow. 'I see. Too delicate a subject for me to handle, is it? Only you three can be trusted to display the sensitivity required?'

Grim smiled. That level of sarcasm wasn't even lost on an ogre. 'Something like that. But when we get to the bottom of it, you'll be the first to know. I promise.'

THE WIZARD AND THE DWARF

Back at The Bollocks, Og-Grim-Dog still had four people to interrogate. But one of them was missing.

'Gurin's off with his friends,' said Sandon when Grim asked where the dwarf was. The wizard had just risen and still looked a little worse for wear.

Og raised a suspicious eyebrow at this news.

'I'll take you to him if you like,' said the wizard. 'I could do with a bit of fresh air and I've a mind to see what bargains I can find in the market with my new wealth.'

The idea of needing fresh air sounded pretty far-fetched to Grim, but he went along with it. Outside, the town of Mer Khazer was busy. Trading was reaching its mid-morning peak, as merchants, peasants and shoppers from the nearby villages and farms had arrived in town to sell their wares and spend their coins. It was vibrant and noisy, completely unlike the ogre's cavern back home. Grim was surprised that he didn't mind the bustling to and fro of town life as much. It was something you could get used to.

'This way,' said Sandon, navigating a path through the crowds.

Og gave Grim a meaningful stare. Now they had Sandon on his own, it was time to interrogate the wizard.

'We were told to pass this on to you,' said Og, producing the ring they had been given by the clerk at the Magical Items desk. 'Ring of Curse Breaking, they said.'

'Ah,' said the wizard, taking the ring and studying it, before placing it on his finger. 'That was all, was it?'

'Yes,' said Grim. He thought about what Mr Agassi had said about the falling incomes from dungeoneering. 'We didn't win so much loot, did we?'

'More than most are making these days.' Sandon looked about him before leaning in and talking more quietly. 'But no, not nearly as much as we used to. Actually, Assata and I put in a complaint to the Bureau yesterday. Some of those dungeons should never have been open to adventurers. And that shop in Wight's Hollow.' He shook his head. 'Not sure how much longer things can go on like this.'

They stopped outside a tavern called The Squished Plums.

'This is where Gurin meets the other dwarves,' Sandon said.

'The other dwarves?'

'Yes. There are several on the circuit. They tend to meet here when they're not adventuring.'

'I see. Thanks, wizard.'

Sandon gave a little wave and carried on down the street.

'Well?' Og asked his brothers as they loitered outside the inn.

'I'm not sure it's him,' said Grim. 'If he was behind the attacks on Darkspike Dungeon and Urlay village, why would he be complaining to the Bureau and asking for the dungeons to be shut down? That doesn't seem to make much sense.'

'And does he really have what it takes to carry out a deception like this?' asked Dog. 'I mean, he's nice enough, but he's hardly dazzled us with his powers, has he?'

'That's true,' said Grim, thinking of all the times on their adventure when Sandon nearly did something useful.

'Unless that was all an elaborate ruse,' Og suggested. 'Alright, maybe not,' he admitted upon seeing his brothers' expressions. 'But what about Gurin? He's a different kettle of fish.'

Grim nodded. 'Bitter about the changes to dungeon crawling in recent years. That might have led him to do something drastic.'

'Plus, he's a dwarf,' said Dog. 'You can't trust—'

'Dog!' said Og, his voice rising threateningly. 'Hasn't this experience taught you anything about judging people?'

Dog seemed to think about it. 'I don't think so.'

Grim acted quickly before a full-blooded argument ensued. He barged through the doors of The Squished Plums and looked about. Dwarves are not generally the easiest of creatures to find, but he spotted half a dozen of them sat around a table in the corner, six tankards in front of them. He marched over. Grim had honestly never seen a more miserable looking collection of faces, and he lived in a dungeon with trolls.

'This is Og-Grim-Dog,' said Gurin, his voice rough but not unfriendly. 'Pull up a chair, ogre.'

Grim turned around to the next table. Og and Dog grabbed separate chairs and there followed a ridiculous tussle over which chair would get placed on the table with the dwarves. Eventually, Grim was able to sit down.

'Og-Grim-Dog, these are my good friends. I've known all of them for half a lifetime, some more.' Gurin gestured to his right. 'This is Hurin.' Hurin raised his pipe at Og-Grim-Dog before taking a puff. 'This old rascal is Durin,' Gurin continued, moving around the circle. 'Then you have Thurin, Kurin, and Tony.'

'Nice to meet you all,' said Grim.

'Unfortunately, you've caught us in a bad mood,' said Gurin.

'What a surprise,' Dog said under his breath.

'You know I've not been happy with the direction of things under the Bureau. But this is another thing entirely. It's more than the last straw. It's an insult that dwarves will not soon forget. Thurin, show the ogre the new form.'

Thurin slid over a piece of paper entitled Membership Equal Opportunities Form REGEQ6. *Not another bloody form*, Grim thought, but reluctantly he scanned it over. It appeared that members of the Bureau now had to complete a check box form, identifying such personal details as race, gender, class and disability.

Og placed a big finger next to the race column.

'No ogres on the list, of course,' he said darkly.

'Look who else isn't on the list,' said Thurin.

Then Grim saw it. 'No dwarves? I don't understand.'

'Look under disabilities.'

The disabilities column was an alphabetical list of ailments, both physical and mental. Under 'D' was dwarfism. Grim looked at it, a little dumbfounded.

'Yes,' confirmed Gurin. 'According to the Bureau, dwarves are no longer a race. We are a disability. This insult won't be allowed to stand, mark my words.'

Gurin's friends growled their agreement. Whatever the rights and wrongs of it, there was no doubting that these adventurers had been offended to their core.

'If you're friends,' began Dog, 'why don't you go adventuring together? And can the Bureau stop you?'

'A proper dungeon crawl,' explained Gurin, 'always used to require a mix of skills. Swords and sorcery; healing and guile; elves, dwarves and humans. You couldn't succeed without brawn; without magic; without dwarven know-how. So, we rarely adventured together. We joined parties and when it was done, we'd come back to the Plums and share our stories and wisdom. This was our life, you understand? And as for adventuring alone, could the Bureau stop us hitting a dungeon? Do they have the resources to police all those locations? Of course not.'

'Half of those dungeons we visited were easy takes,' Dog said. 'So there's nothing to stop you doing it yourselves.'

'But we don't want to do that,' Gurin seethed. 'We want our world back. We want it to be the same as it used to be.'

THE ELF

Og-Grim-Dog stayed for a drink with the dwarves but then decided to leave them to pick over their grievances. After all, there were still two members of the group they had yet to speak with.

Back at The Bollocks, they found Raya in the bar.

'Ah,' she called over. 'I'm all by myself here. Come and have a drink with me.'

The ogre's stomachs rumbled. 'Do they do food here?' Dog asked.

'Food? Even better idea!' Raya said enthusiastically. 'I know the perfect place. Come on.'

No sooner had Og-Grim-Dog returned to the inn than they found themselves leaving again, for yet another part of town. Raya the elf took them to a side street, away from the crowds. The street was narrow, the buildings on either side leaning towards each other precariously, blocking almost all the light. Grim only took a couple of paces down the street before he smelt the aroma of sizzling meat and spices.

'Faster, Grim,' said Dog, his mouth drooling.

Halfway down the street, Raya led them into an anonymous looking building. Inside it was poorly lit and dingy looking. A dining area in front of them led on to the cooking area at the back of the room, from where the noise and smell of frying food wafted. The tables seemed to be sprawled about the dining area with no thought. There were no chairs, just benches and boxes to sit on. Not the kind of place Grim would have thought an elf would choose to go for lunch. But for an ogre, it was perfect.

'Welcome to Sheev's,' said the elf.

They took a table. Og reached out for a menu, but Raya snatched it away.

'You *have* to order the chilli burger and fries,' she insisted, with an emotional intensity.

'Alright, Raya,' Og agreed.

She smiled and went to the bar to give the order.

'What about the elf?' Dog asked while she was out of earshot.

'She hides things,' said Grim. 'I bet she wouldn't want Assata to know she'd come here, for example.'

'Everybody hides something,' said Og.

'I don't!' said Dog.

'We both hide under sacks when Grim goes walking in human lands,' Og said. For once, he didn't say it in an argumentative way, and for once Dog didn't try to dispute the point, simply grunting an acknowledgement.

'All in all,' said Grim, 'I would say she's the least likely of the lot to be secretly killing humans disguised as an orc.'

His brothers nodded in reluctant agreement.

Raya returned to the table, an excited look on her face.

'Raya,' said Grim. 'We have something odd to show you.'

He knew his brothers would agree. Dog took out the sword.

'This was in the returns we picked up from the Magical Items box,' Og said.

The elf frowned. 'What, you mean identical to the one you found in Urlay?'

In answer, Og withdrew the original from his belt.

'The clerk was sure it was with the things we handed in.'

'I told everyone to put their special finds in that bag,' she said. 'They knew I was taking them to Magical Items.'

'Why would they have one of these orc swords in their possession and not tell the rest of us?' asked Grim.

Raya made a face. 'There aren't many explanations. You're suggesting that someone in our party was involved in the attack on Urlay?'

'How well do you know the others?'

'I've known Sandon and Gurin a very long time. Assata and Brother Kane started adventuring more recently.' She paused. 'I've known you for a couple of weeks.'

'Well, it's not us!' said Dog, affronted.

Raya shrugged. 'Just making a point.'

'Where has Brother Kane gone?' Grim asked her.

'When the Brother is not adventuring, he spends his time tending to the needs of the more unfortunate in the town. You can often find him at the orphanage. Why, you suspect him?'

'Well, we've investigated everyone else already.'

'Oh, that's what this is, is it?' asked the elf, looking hurt. 'I thought you *wanted* to go out to lunch with me.'

'We did!' said Grim. 'We knew it wasn't you.'

'And why couldn't it be me?' Raya demanded, apparently equally offended.

'You're...' Og began, then struggled for the right words.

Oh dear, thought Grim. Diplomacy wasn't a strength of either of his brothers.

'...too nice.'

Well. It could have been worse.

'Huh. Maybe I should work on that.'

'Og can give you a few lessons on being a mean bastard,' said Dog, then barked with laughter.

Og shot his brother a dirty look.

'I never really felt like I belonged in elvish society,' Raya admitted, suddenly candid. 'Too haughty. And too much salad. I suppose I make an extra effort to get on with people here. Maybe too much effort sometimes.'

'Well, we know how that feels,' said Grim. 'Ogres are solitary creatures by nature.'

'But you're not solitary. I mean, you have each other.'

'Yes,' said Grim. 'But we don't really have a choice about that, do we?'

Raya chuckled. 'I suppose not. Anyway, what were we talking about?'

'About Brother Kane. If he's at the orphanage, how can we investigate him without making it look obvious? Besides, we're liable to scare the children.'

Raya pursed her lips, then rustled in her pockets. She produced an amulet, hanging on a silver chain, and handed it over. Og-Grim-Dog looked in awe at the artwork: vivid blue, green and yellow colouring depicted moons and stars.

'An elven Amulet of Hiding,' Raya said. 'If you place it around your neck it will make you invisible and silent. Be careful, though. It's never a good idea to use magic too frequently, even magic stored in charms such as this.'

The waiter appeared with their meals. Og and Dog tucked into their burgers.

'Oh Grim,' Og said in a voice full of wonder, picking up the third burger, 'you have to try this.'

A taste explosion hit Grim as he took his first bite of meatiness and fiery sauce. 'This is delicious,' he got out between chews. 'What is it made from?'

Raya put a finger to her lips. 'We don't ask questions about the chilli burgers, Grim. We just eat them.'

THE CLERIC

Og-Grim-Dog walked through the streets of Mer Khazer, concealed by the Amulet of Hiding. They tested its powers at first, unsure what precisely Raya had meant by invisible and silent. Dog leaned over and screamed at a passer-by, who didn't flinch or respond at all to the noise. Grim found that being invisible could actually make moving around more difficult. Other pedestrians seemed to see open space where in fact there was ogre. He did his best to avoid people but was too slow to get out of the way of one fast-moving young man, who ended up flattened on the street, a bemused expression on his face.

Eventually, they located the orphanage of Mer Khazer. It was a solid-looking, stone-built house over two floors. A plaque outside thanked the adventurers of Mer Khazer who had paid for its construction. Grim wondered how they were going to negotiate their way in through the rather narrow-looking door. Because while they were silent and invisible, they weren't any smaller, and the residents might not react well to an invisible monster entering the property.

He was relieved, therefore, when Og overheard the noise of children playing in the back and directed him there. Of course, the orphans were outside. The orphanage had a large green behind it where the children of the town congregated. A crowd of them had gathered on the grass, and in amongst them all was Brother Kane.

Grim walked closer to get a better view of what the priest was up to. He had several sacks with him, and the ogre watched as he dipped his hand into one of them, producing a hobby-horse which he gave to one of the girls, who promptly rode off on the toy, galloping about and making neighing noises. Brother Kane had a gift for each child: balls, puppets, hoops, dolls, toy knights, toy boats, spinning tops, rattles for the babes. He made sure each child received a toy and when he was done with the gift giving, stayed to play games with the children, his beatific smile never leaving his face. He gently settled disputes and dried tears when the inevitable happened and a toy was broken or lost within minutes of being received, replacing it with something else from one of his sacks.

'So that's what he did with his share of the loot,' said Og as they watched the scene play out, still hidden by elven magic.

'Doesn't look like he's our murderer,' Grim said.

'Could be an act,' said Dog, unconvinced.

'Oh come on,' countered Og. 'That's ridiculous.'

'Is it? If you were an evil bastard trying to cover your tracks, isn't this exactly the kind of thing you would do?'

'So everyone who helps other people is automatically suspicious? What a sad world you live in.'

'I didn't say that,' Dog shouted.

'Please don't start—' Grim began, then stopped. 'Wait, where is he going now?'

'Aha!' Dog crowed. 'Follow him, Grim!'

Brother Kane said his fond farewells to the children of Mer Khazer and walked across the green. Grim followed him, heading down one of the streets that led back into town. The cleric crossed to a residential street, walked a bit farther on, then walked up a path to a house. He knocked on the door, waited a short while, then the door opened, and he was invited inside.

Grim walked up to the house and studied it. It was a nondescript, wattle and daub affair, just the same as the other houses all along the street. There was no plaque outside to tell them who lived there.

A couple walked past them.

'Do you know who lives here?' Grim asked them.

The couple walked on as if he hadn't said a word.

'Oh, I forgot about that damned amulet,' said Grim. 'Take it off will you, Og?'

The sudden appearance of a three-headed ogre from out of nowhere caused everyone in the vicinity to scream, turn around and run away. Everyone except one stern, older woman, who had the look of someone who'd seen a lot worse than magically appearing ogres. She approached them and began wagging her finger.

'You'd better not be about to feast on those inside there,' she warned. 'My mother lives here!'

'This is your mother's house?'

'It's not *her* house. It's a home for the elderly.'

Grim sighed. 'So first he visits an orphanage, then an old people's home. I think we've seen enough of Brother Kane to tick him off our list.'

Dog made a sceptical sounding grunt. 'We just haven't uncovered his dark secrets yet, that's all.'

'What now?' Og asked. 'We haven't got very much out of following them all over town.'

Grim thought about it. 'You're right, Og. I think we need to go back to Urlay.'

'The village that was attacked? What's the point in going back there, Grim?'

'I think we're missing something. Some piece of evidence that we haven't noticed.'

And with that, Grim began to march for Urlay.

GRIM SOLVES THE CASE

Grim knew they were close to solving the case. If you were to ask him why he was so committed to getting to the truth, he might have struggled to explain it. But one of the reasons, surely, was that no-one expected an ogre to do it. Ogres, it was generally agreed, were stupid brutes. Somewhere deep down, beneath his conscious thought, he wanted to prove them wrong.

He used human roads; he tracked across heath and moorland; retracing routes that the adventurers had taken on their way to and from dungeons. Beside him, Og and Dog had their heads covered. One slept, the other muttered incessantly, an endless stream of complaints that Grim easily ignored.

They slept in the open, each brother taking a turn at keeping watch, waking the next when it was his turn. Grim didn't doubt that many eyes observed their progress, watching from dark places; high places; secret places. What mattered was that none impeded their progress, and in the end, he found himself walking down into the valley where the village of Urlay stood by the river.

'You can take the bags off now,' he said, and his brothers reappeared, eyes screwed up as they adjusted to the sudden introduction of light.

They wandered past the first houses. Those nearest the river were the ones that had been attacked. Some had been left with minor damage: others, those where fire had taken hold, were little more than charred remains. Og-Grim-Dog inspected the buildings. Grim's brothers were quiet, respecting the fact that they were looking at what had been people's homes. But they found nothing. With a feeling of inevitability, Grim found himself returning to the inn. If they were going to find anything, it would be at The Crushed Grapes.

Dog pushed the door open.

'No-one around,' he muttered, and Grim entered the lounge area. It was quiet, not even a clanging from the kitchen this time. Would the folk of the village still be cowering down in the cellar? Well, if they were, they would hear Grim creaking the floorboards—there was no point in an ogre trying to be quiet.

Grim looked about, thinking. He walked over to the bar, and then around it, taking the step up to stand behind it. Here he could look out towards the front yard and the river.

Og reached for a tankard. 'It's fun back here. Imagine if we were a landlord, eh Grim?'

But Grim was still thinking. 'The landlady. Betty. Said she looked out from behind the bar, and she caught a glimpse of the heads of the orcs. That's when they all hid down in the cellar.'

'You've got a good memory, Grim,' said Dog, filling Og's tankard for him.

'I know we're a good deal bigger than Betty,' Grim continued. 'But don't you think she'd see a bit more than their heads from here?'

His brothers looked out to the river.

'Maybe,' Og conceded. 'Hard to tell.'

Grim grunted in acknowledgement. He left the bar area, walked back to the middle of the lounge, and took a deep breath.

'Hello?' he shouted. 'It's Og-Grim-Dog here. The ogre from a few days back? You probably remember us. We mean you no harm. Is Betty about?'

There was the sound of movement from down below, and then a door being pushed open. Footsteps. Betty appeared from the direction of the kitchen.

'What do you want?' she asked suspiciously.

*

Somehow, Grim persuaded Betty to help them. But he needed more than just Betty, so she called to the children down in the cellar. They appeared, gawping at the three-headed ogre who stood in their home. Grim was pleased to see that they came in all shapes and sizes, from a toddler who only reached to his knees, to a girl who had reached the height of Betty.

Once they got going, the children started to enjoy the process. Grim had them march, one at a time, along the riverbank. As they did, Betty looked out from her position from behind the bar. Each time a child walked past, she told Og-Grim-Dog what she could see.

'Top of Nath's head. Lydia, shoulders and up. Nothing. Harry's head.'

When it was done, the children were called back in. Grim thanked them. Og gave Betty a purse full of coin. The villagers of Urlay would need it more than them.

'So, young Harry here was the height of the orcs you saw?'

'Yes,' said Betty, falteringly. 'I'm sure of it, but it doesn't make sense. He's but twelve years old.'

'And they were all the same size? Each one, it was just their head you could see?'

'Aye. I can see it clearly, in my mind's eye.'

'Wait a minute,' said Dog, only now paying attention to Grim's little experiment. 'The orcs you saw were all this size?' He put his hand parallel to the top of Harry's head. The boy only came up to the ogre's hip. 'They weren't no orcs, then. They were dwarves. But that means—'

'Yes,' said Grim. 'It was Gurin.'

'Dwarves did this?' Betty asked. 'Why?'

'I'm not sure. But we're going to go back to Mer Khazer now. Those dwarves have some questions to answer.'

'Thank you. Here, let me get you something for the journey,' she said, leaving for the kitchen. While they waited, Og and Dog gave the children rides. The children took turns sitting in the ogre's great hands, who then shot their arms up at full speed, taking care not to slam the kids into the ceiling. Betty came back with a loaf of bread, a big slab of cheese and a little bag of vegetables.

Dog took the food, looking a little emotional at the gift. They said their goodbyes to the children of Urlay and Betty led them out of The Crushed Grapes.

Outside, Grim heard human voices. Out on the river, a group of barges were heading for the jetty. They were full of armed men.

'Oh dear,' said Betty. 'It'll be Deston, the reeve of Dorwich City. He has a fearsome reputation. I think you should go—quickly. They might not understand what you're doing here.'

Sure enough, shouts of alarm and anger carried to them from the river, as the soldiers on the barges spotted the ogre with the woman.

'Goodbye,' said Og-Grim-Dog, before turning away and walking back through the village. Grim retraced their steps, passing the houses of the villagers one last time before beginning the climb up from the valley floor. The shouts of hostility from the river didn't stop. Og looked back over his shoulder.

'They're getting off their boats,' he said. 'Looks like they're going to chase us.'

'Let them,' said Dog. 'I'm in the mood for a fight.'

'There's far too many, Dog,' Grim chided. An idea suddenly struck him. 'Put on Raya's amulet, will you?'

Dog reluctantly did as he asked, and the ogre became both invisible and silent.

'That should make following us a little more difficult,' Grim said. He relaxed a little, concentrating on making the return journey to Mer Khazer.

THE REEVE OF MER KHAZER

Once more, Og-Grim-Dog found themselves passing through the gates of Mer Khazer. Their mood was sombre, because although they had liked Gurin the dwarf, they knew they had to confront him over his actions.

Grim had the time to think about their approach during the return journey from Urlay. Challenging Gurin alone, he decided, wasn't a great idea. Gurin was a hot head, as was Dog, and the chances of violence would be high. He would prefer to avoid bloodshed. So, when they got back to The Bruised Bollocks, he called a meeting of their party. Sandon and Raya helped him to fetch everyone, and it wasn't long before the six of them were reunited in the tap room of The Bollocks.

'What's this all about?' Assata asked. 'Where have you been?'

'It's time to come clean. There was a reason we came to Mer Khazer,' Grim began. 'We aimed to find out why Darkspike Dungeon was being attacked so frequently by adventurers. We thought that joining your crew would help us to find the answers we were looking for. We felt like we were getting close to solving the puzzle. So we returned to Urlay,' he added, finding it hard not to take a quick glance at Gurin's troubled expression.

'After finding this amongst our dungeon winnings,' said Og, laying one of the orc swords on the table.

'Another one?' Sandon asked.

'Yes. Same as this,' said Dog, placing the second next to it.

'You can see,' Grim resumed, 'that the blade has the broad-headed shape common to orc swords. But the hilt is quite different to orcish weapons, more skilfully crafted than you would expect from orcs. In Urlay, we conducted an experiment with the landlady of The Crushed Grapes. Betty. We identified the height of the 'orcs' that she had seen by the river.'

'They were this high,' said Dog, putting his hand to his hip. 'Dwarf size.'

'Alright,' said Gurin. He wasn't as angry as Grim had expected. There was an air of resignation about him. 'I can see you've got all the evidence you need. It was us.'

'Us?' Assata asked.

'Me, Hurin, Durin, Thurin, Kurin and Tony.'

'We worked out it was you who attacked Urlay,' said Grim. 'I'm not sure why you did it, though.'

Gurin sighed. 'The Bureau. We just got sick of it. All the rules and regulations. The last straw was when they started turning down applications to dungeons, saying they were too weak for a dungeon crawl. A dungeon full of monsters, and the Bureau is taking their side over its members? What kind of lunacy is that? Anyway. We found a way round the ban. If there were reports of bands of orcs targeting human settlements, the Bureau would open up the local dungeons.'

'So you killed humans,' said Raya, sounding angry, 'so that you could keep killing orcs and goblins?'

'Hang on now, Raya. We didn't kill any humans.'

'How do you know that? You fired their homes. If no-one died after what you did, it's only out of luck.'

'I know. When you put it like that, we did wrong. I see that.'

'You saw those dungeons we visited,' Sandon added. 'Wight's Hollow and the rest. You've just made the situation worse. More dungeons will be closed now, thanks to you.'

'I know, wizard, I know. But I had one last hurrah, didn't I? After all, dwarves aren't even a race anymore, according to the Bureau. We've been all but pushed out already. The life we knew, the world that meant everything to us, has been taken away. So what did I have to lose?'

Brother Kane gave Gurin a beatific smile and withdrew his vial of holy water. 'I forgive you, my son.'

'Never mind that,' said Assata, slapping the cleric's arm. 'We're handing this murderer in to the authorities. And the other five as well. You need to face justice for what you've done, Gurin.'

The dwarf didn't argue. They took him to see the reeve of Mer Khazer, who was in charge of law and order in the town.

'Hassletoff is a veteran adventurer himself,' Sandon explained as they cut through the streets to the reeve's office. Gurin walked with them, showing no signs of wishing to make a run for it, though Assata kept a hand near her sword hilt just in case. 'Well respected by our community, we helped him gain the office when he decided his adventuring days were done.'

Sandon knocked on the door of the reeve's office and when it opened a halfling appeared. He appraised them coolly. Hassletoff was even smaller than Gurin, but he held himself with a relaxed kind of confidence. The sword at his belt gave him a serious look and his moustache made him look a little older than his boyish features would suggest by themselves.

'I don't like the look of this,' he said at last.

'Indeed, Hassletoff,' said Sandon sadly. The wizard proceeded to tell the reeve all that Gurin was accused of. When he was done, the halfling led the dwarf into his office and secured him in a locked cell.

'You can leave him with me,' he told them when he returned. 'The justice system will soon get to work, and he'll be given a fair trial.'

'He has five accomplices,' Assata told him. 'All dwarves. They're probably still in The Squished Plums. If you go now, you can get them while they're all together.'

The reeve stroked at his moustache as he considered her words. 'Very well. I'm making you my deputies. You're coming with me.'

'Wait a minute,' said Og. 'I'm not comfortable working for the rozzers.'

'It's not a request,' the reeve responded sharply, no sign of feeling intimidated by the bulk of the ogre. 'I have the authority to make anyone my deputy. I suggest you co-operate, unless you want to join Gurin in my cell.'

'Do we get a badge?' asked Dog hopefully.

*

The reeve ordered Og-Grim-Dog into The Squished Plums. Alone. The others were positioned around the building, covering any possible exit. Og wasn't happy that they were the ones sent in to do the dirty work. Dog was excited about seeing some action. Grim just wanted it over with. For while he supposed that the dwarves did deserve to be punished, he didn't want to kill anyone.

Grim ran inside, heading for the table where he had met the dwarves the other day. He was lucky. All five were seated around the table, drinks in front of them. Although Gurin had introduced them to him, Grim had no idea which dwarf was which: he couldn't even remember their names. One of them puffed on a pipe, while the others appeared to be in the midst of some complaint-filled conversation, their brows furrowed with discontent.

Grim didn't slow, getting to the table before the dwarves realised what was happening. Dog reached over and grabbed one of them, lifting him into the air. Og picked up a second.

'Help!' shouted the dwarf who dangled in Dog's grip. 'Hurin, help me!'

The three remaining dwarves stared wide-eyed with shock for a split second, before they leapt from their chairs. One of them approached Grim and kicked him in the shins with his heavy boot.

'Ow!' Grim complained. It was painful and he was more than a little annoyed.

The dwarf kicked him again, in the same spot.

'Look!' Grim demanded. 'Kicking me isn't going to make Og or Dog release your friends, is it?'

The dwarf made a confused face.

'Run away!' shouted the dwarf that had been caught by Og. 'Escape while you can!'

The three free dwarves all turned and ran, making for different exits from the inn. Grim followed one of them to the rear entrance.

'Oi!' Dog shouted at his captive. 'Stop biting!' He clunked the dwarf into the wall of the inn in an effort to make him stop.

Grim left the inn. Outside, Assata had wrestled one of the dwarves to the floor and locked its arm behind its back.

'Up!' she demanded, pulling on the arm, and the third dwarf reluctantly got to its feet.

They skirted around the building, looking for the others. Success. Hassletoff had a sword pointed at the fourth dwarf. Raya had an arrow fixed on the fifth. Sandon and Brother Kane stood with her, though it was unclear what help they had been.

'The reeve nodded at them. 'Well done, deputies. Come on, let's go. I have enough room in my cells for them all.'

THE REEVE OF DORWICH CITY

They stood together outside the reeve's office. Grim sensed the sadness in the group. Raya and Sandon had known Gurin and the other dwarves for a long time. It was a shame it had ended like this. But they had attacked innocents, and it was hard to argue that they didn't deserve to be punished.

'What will happen to them?' he asked into the silence.

The others looked at one another, until their eyes rested on Hassletoff.

The reeve sighed. 'If the court finds them guilty of murder, then it's a death sentence.'

'Anything less and it's a fine,' Sandon said, adding a note of optimism.

'Well,' said Grim, feeling a little awkward. 'We came here to find out why our dungeon was being attacked so frequently. We've discovered the reason, and hopefully, put a stop to it. I guess it's time for us to go back home.'

'I'll miss you,' said Raya. Before the ogre realised what was happening, the elf was hugging them, Og and Dog gently patting her head and shoulders.

'Here,' said Dog, his voice sounding emotional. He held out Raya's amulet.

'You keep it,' she said. 'You might need it.'

Then the others said their farewells, too. Assata banged fists with Og.

'Fight the power,' he told her.

'You know I will.'

Sandon and Hassletoff went for the more traditional shaking of hands, and finally Brother Kane sprinkled water into their faces in a goodbye blessing.

But as it turned out, it was not quite time for Og-Grim-Dog to leave.

A young man came running up the street towards the group. He stopped before them, red-faced and gasping.

'Hassletoff, there's a militia outside the city walls demanding entry. We said we'd fetch you.'

The reeve rolled his eyes. 'Damn, it's one of those days. How many, Oliver? Did you get a name?'

'Must be about fifty. It's Deston, from Dorwich City.'

Uh-oh, Grim said to himself.

'Damn. What does he want?'

The young man raised a shaky arm and pointed it at Og-Grim-Dog. 'They've come for him.'

*

The gossip had spread around Mer Khazer. A large crowd was gathered by the city gates. Grim sensed that the atmosphere was tense. Some of the citizens were clearly worried about letting Deston inside. Others were more pugnacious, ready to stand up to the outsiders.

As the six of them approached, the reeve was bombarded with questions. The citizenry demanded to know what he was going to do.

'Alright, alright,' he said, waving his hands irritably. 'I will talk to them.'

'Oh shit,' said Raya.

A delegation of twenty individuals arrived at the scene. Grim recognised some of them as employees of the Bureau. There was the tall human woman who had originally prevented him from enrolling, and who had delighted in telling him when the constitution had been rewritten to exclude ogres. There was the ineffectual centaur from Non-Human Resources; the witch from Magical Items. These individuals waited in the background as two armour-clad warriors stepped forward, helmets hiding their features, on either side of a sorcerer. He was clad in a black robe, a wooden staff in his hand. He oozed power and authority.

'Barclay,' Sandon said under his breath. 'The Director of the Bureau.'

'Hassletoff?' Barclay demanded, his voice part malice, part resignation at the incompetence of others.

'Director Barclay?'

'I understand that the ogre in your company is wanted for questioning by the authorities of Dorwich City. The Bureau has made it very clear that there is no place for him in our organisation. Please, escort him from the city.'

But, Director Barclay,' Hassletoff objected. 'Only today, Og-Grim-Dog served the city as one of my deputies. It would be unfair to hand him over without any assurances as to his safety.'

Barclay raised one eyebrow. 'Hassletoff, you hold your office based on my recommendation of your fitness to serve. Don't make me withdraw that recommendation.'

'Get the ogre out!' someone from the crowd shouted. Others joined in, demanding that Og-Grim-Dog be expelled from Mer Khazer.

'You cheered for us just days ago!' Og shouted at them angrily, his voice loud enough to silence the crowd. 'What's changed?'

'You see?' Barclay asked, speaking to Hassletoff. 'The monster is a danger. If you can't deal with this, I will have to.'

The two warriors at his side put their hands on the hilts of their swords. Hassletoff copied their move. Assata placed a hand on the halfling's shoulder.

'No. Open the gates. We'll go out with him.'

'But—'

'Getting yourself killed isn't going to solve anything.'

'Don't worry,' Sandon added. 'We've got this.'

Reluctantly, the reeve took his hand from his weapon and ordered the gates to the city opened. They revealed fifty armed humans waiting for them on the other side.

Grim walked through. His four friends followed him.

Dog held up his arm. 'No. This isn't your fight.'

'Don't you dare,' Assata told him, her voice burning with anger. 'Of course it is.'

Dog decided not to argue. Grim smiled to himself. They had never had friends like this before, and it felt good. The five of them walked out and stopped in a line in front of the soldiers of Dorwich City.

'I've got this,' Sandon told them, removing his shoes. Grim got a glimpse of bony toes and long nails that hadn't been cut back in years. 'On the island of Tokaido there is a sect of holy warriors, the Bujutsu, whose learning stretches back centuries. I studied with the wise ones of that creed for two years, learning a deep spirituality, as well as the secrets of their martial prowess. All I need to do is locate the inner peace I discovered on that island, and I will be able to vanquish our enemies with ease.' The wizard began humming to himself.

One of the men took a few steps forward. He was tall and muscular, one of the strongest looking humans Grim had ever seen. He walked with a casual confidence.

'If you didn't know, I'm Deston, the reeve at Dorwich. We're after the ogre,' he said, nodding in the direction of Og-Grim-Dog. 'We've tracked it here from Urlay village. I need to find out what it knows about an attack on the village.'

'The ogre was investigating the attack on Urlay,' said Brother Kane. 'He was not involved in it. We have apprehended the villains responsible in Mer Khazer. They will face justice for that crime.'

Deston smiled pleasantly. 'Interesting. Let me make this clear, cleric: I have a great respect for men of faith. But I will be taking that ogre for interrogation. I am responsible for the defence of the lands about Dorwich; including Urlay. I saw the ogre there with my own eyes. Please, return to your city now. That goes for the rest of you. Let me do my job. I won't ask a second time.'

At these words, Assata drew her sword. She looked across at Raya, who took her bow from her shoulder and strung it. Dog took his mace in his hand, and Og his pike. Brother Kane removed his vial of holy water, fingers hovering above the stopper. Next to him, Sandon continued to hum.

Deston's eyebrows raised, genuinely shocked at the response. 'There's fifty of us—all armed, you fools!' He shook his head. 'So be it. I gave you fair warning.' He signalled to his men. They raised their shields and hefted their spears. Grim looked at the faces. Some grinned, some were expressionless. Not a single one of them looked nervous.

Suddenly, there was a high-pitched scream, and a figure flew in the air towards the nearest of Deston's soldiers. It was Sandon.

What followed was one of the strangest things Grim had ever witnessed.

The wizard moved so fast that Deston's men were unable to react. A foot crunched into the head of the soldier, but already Sandon's other foot was kicking the man next to him. So it went on, the wizard's feet running from one enemy to the next, while his body remained airborne. His legs moved faster than Grim had thought possible, kicking out, snapping heads back, sending armed men crashing to the floor. His big toes found their way into eyes and up nostrils. Should a soldier manage to dodge one foot, the second clobbered into them, sending them sprawling. Deston found his head locked between two bony shins, before Sandon flipped him over and over, until he hit the ground. Finally, when every single soldier had been sent to the floor, Sandon returned to his starting position.

They all looked at him, open-mouthed. Sandon placed his palms together and bowed. 'That took me back. But as they say on Tokaido—once a Bujutsu, always a Bujutsu.'

Grim strode towards Deston. The reeve found the blade of Og's pike at his neck.

'We were at Urlay investigating the orcish attack on the village,' Grim told him. 'We have identified and apprehended the culprits. So, there really is no need for your posse to stay in the field. You can return to Dorwich City, reassured that the danger is gone, and justice is served.'

Deston eyed the pike at his neck. 'Of course. Apologies for being slow to understand. We will return to Dorwich immediately.'

Grim nodded, satisfied, and Og withdrew the weapon. They watched as Deston's men got to their feet, and the reeve led them away from the city.

'Well, that was a fun way to end our little adventure,' Grim said to his friends. 'But now I think it really is time to return to Darkspike Dungeon.'

'I am sorry we won't be dungeoneering with you again,' Sandon told them. 'Unfortunately, I fear there are dark forces at the Bureau, who will always seek to work against you. Until we can mount a proper challenge to them, you will have enemies in Mer Khazer.'

'That's alright,' said Og. 'For a little while I enjoyed being a hero. But today I learned that it's an illusion. The people can be turned against you.'

'Not all the people,' said Assata. 'The ones who matter will always remember you.'

BACK HOME

Things were soon back to the way they had always been at Darkspike Dungeon. Queen Krim and the orcs recovered from the depredations of the trespassers, until one day she even felt strong enough to send out a small raiding party.

Og-Grim-Dog could enjoy their dank cavern in peace, so long as they ignored the noise from the kobolds upstairs. In fact, it was so peaceful, that the brothers were pleased to see Gary the goblin when he arrived at their home once more. He had come to deliver a letter, and after a polite chat, the ogre sat itself on the floor and settled down to read the words.

It was quite lengthy, and Og was the only brother who could read it easily.

WRITTEN AT THE BRUISED BOLLOCKS

DEAR OG-GRIM-DOG,

I HOPE YOU ARE ENJOYING YOUR 'RETIREMENT' FROM DUNGEONEERING. I

THOUGHT YOU MIGHT LIKE TO HEAR OUR NEWS FROM MER KHAZER.

THE BIG STORY IS THE ESCAPE OF GURIN 'FUCKAXE' AND HIS DWARVEN FRIENDS FROM TOFF'S CELLS. THERE WAS A NIGHT-TIME BREAK-IN AND ALL SIX DWARVES WERE SPRUNG. IT TURNS OUT THERE WAS A SEVENTH DWARF LOOSE IN THE CITY—SEVEN DWARVES! I GUESS WE SHOULD HAVE KNOWN!

'I don't get it,' said Dog. 'Why should we have known there were seven dwarves?'

'I don't know, Dog,' said Grim. 'Probably an elven joke. They have a weird sense of humour. Carry on, Og.'

GURIN AND HIS FRIENDS LEFT THE CITY, NO-ONE KNOWS WHERE TO. I'M NOT REALLY SURE WHAT TO THINK ABOUT IT, BUT A PART OF ME IS GLAD THAT GURIN GOT AWAY.

THE ADVENTURING LIFE HASN'T CHANGED THAT MUCH. THERE AREN'T ANY DWARF HEROES ANYMORE, WHICH MAKES THINGS A BIT MORE CHALLENGING. THE

DUNGEONS AREN'T QUITE AS 'SOFT' AS THEY WERE, EITHER, NOW THAT THE FAKE ORC RAIDS HAVE STOPPED. BUT THE BUREAU IS STILL THE SAME. ASSATA AND SANDON TALK DARKLY OF 'DEALING' WITH IT. THEY SEND THEIR LOVE BY THE WAY, AS DOES BROTHER KANE.

I HAD A CHILLI BURGER AND FRIES AT SHEEV'S TODAY AND THOUGHT OF YOU. HENCE THE LETTER.

WELL, THAT'S IT FROM ME. SMELL YA LATER,

RAYA S

'So, Gurin escaped, eh?' said Og. 'I'm with the elf. Not sure what to think about that.'

'Good luck to him, I say,' said Dog.

'It was nice of Raya to write us,' said Grim. 'The human lands are a confusing place. All those people running around, trying to live their busy little lives. And all of them with just the one head each. Makes me think it must be lonely. Makes me think—' Grim paused. Ogres didn't do emotions, but a strange feeling had come over him. 'Makes me think I'm lucky to have you two for company.'

Og and Dog nodded, clearing their throats awkwardly.

'Yes, well,' said Dog gruffly. 'Listening to that letter made me hungry. How are we doing for bones?'

'I think we have plenty,' said Og. 'Come on, Grim, let's take a look.'

Grim got to his feet. He took a step towards their pile of bones in the corner, but then stopped.

'I don't want to,' he said.

'What?' Dog demanded. 'You fancy fresh meat tonight?'

'No. I don't want us to spend the rest of our lives at the bottom of this dungeon, gnawing on bones. I want us to go on more adventures, while we still can. Alright, maybe we're not suited to being heroes. Maybe it's too soon for three-headed ogres to be accepted. But that doesn't mean we have to stay down here. Hiding from the world.'

'Hiding?' demanded Dog. 'I'm not hiding from nothing.'

'Alright, Grim,' said Og. 'If it's adventures you want, I'm game. After all, it's you who has to do all the walking.'

'What do you say, Dog?' Grim asked.

'I won't have it said I'm holding us back from a fight. Let's do it.'

Og-Grim-Dog put their possessions into a travelling pack and put their weapons on their belt. They left their cavern. They walked past rooms full of goblins, who peered at them suspiciously. They stopped to say goodbye to Queen Krim, Sovereign and Despot of the Black Orcs. Then they left Darkspike Dungeon behind them and went into the Great Outside.

THE END OF THE MIDDLE

The Recorder made his final flourishes. The Flayed Testicles was deadly silent, save for the scratch of quill on parchment. When he was done, he opened a pouch and sprinkled sand onto the fresh ink.

The three heads of the Landlord, and the many heads of his customers, stared intently at the small form perched near the bar. Seemingly oblivious of their attention, the Recorder shook out the stiffness from his hand and then rubbed at his sore wrist.

'Well?' the third head of the ogre demanded, his patience exhausted. 'I shouldn't have to remind you that your life, and the life of everyone here, is at stake. Do you claim that those marks you have made on your pages accurately portray our story?'

'I believe so,' said the Recorder with confidence.

Some in the Testicles relaxed a little, but others knew better. For their Landlord had yet to give his approval.

'Then we have only one question,' said the third head, a sly smile on his face. 'The tale we told tonight wasn't the most glorious episode in our lives we could have shared. But you could say it was the most important. If you are truly a master of your craft, you will know why we chose it. Why did we really start in the middle?'

The customers of the inn frowned at one another in confusion. Why *did* their Landlord begin the story of his life at the middle? It had been a strange decision. In the quiet and peaceable realm of Magidu, stories always started at the beginning and carried on until the end.

'Because,' the Recorder replied in a clear voice, 'this was the moment when you chose to live. The moment when you chose danger and adventure over safety and familiarity. Thus, all the infamous deeds of Og-Grim-Dog can be traced back to your time in Mer Khazer: to your decision to leave your dungeon; to a letter written by an elf; to the friends you made.'

The Landlord stared at the Recorder for a while. The customers of the inn could see different expressions on his three faces: they could see disappointment and respect and relief. Finally, the middle head spoke.

'You are wise, Recorder. Wiser than you seem. And you have earned the right to record our story for posterity. Same time tomorrow?'

'Alright,' said the Recorder, who began to pack up his equipment.

'You'll like tomorrow's story,' said the first head, a vicious looking grin appearing on his face. 'No more Mr Nice Guys.'

END CREDITS

The customers of The Flayed Testicles spilled out onto the streets, ready to stagger back to their homes. As the fresh air hit them, a wave of relief struck with it. They had made it out alive.

Then the shadow of the Landlord loomed in the doorway behind them. Reluctantly, they turned to look.

'And a nice review wouldn't go amiss,' suggested the ogre.

***

Thanks to my beta readers: Lisa Maughan, Lana Turner, Marcus Nilsson & Ian Edmundson.

Thanks to everyone else who has supported my work. Two special thank yous for this one. Vivien Edmundson, for inviting Og-Grim-Dog to The Wayfarer (which has since changed its name to The Bruised Bollocks) & alpha-reader Michael Evan, who believed in this project from the beginning.

CONNECT WITH THE AUTHOR

Subscribe to Jamie's newsletter to claim your free digital copy of the prequel to The Weapon Takers Saga, *Striking Out*

https://subscribe.jamieedmundson.com/

Website:

jamieedmundson.com

Twitter:

@jamie_edmundson

Og-Grim-Dog and The Dark Lord

Find out whether the three-headed ogre has more success as a villain, in the second novel of the Me Three series.

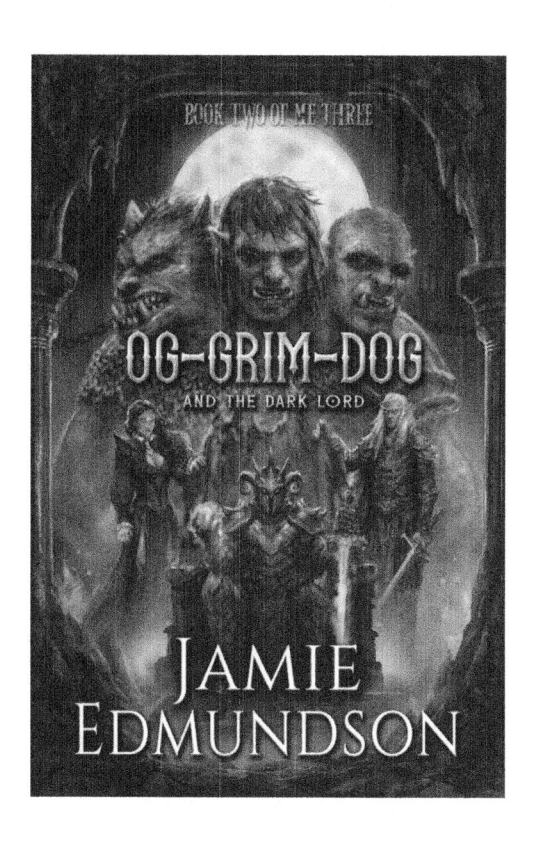

Printed in Great Britain
by Amazon